# More praise for
# HOLE IN THE WATER

"[An] electrifying thriller . . . Kearney is gifted at setting his scenes and creating suspense. . . . You're in for a dynamite story about shame, revenge, and the desperate desire to escape one's past."
—Detroit Free Press

"Robert Kearney has written a spine-tingling work of psychological suspense and terror, made all the more frightening because the story line is locked into an all-too-real world. . . . *Hole in the Water* makes our worst nightmares feel like children's dreams. For that reason alone, this is one book worth buying at any price."
—BookPage

"A hard, bloody tale, rendered with grisly accuracy. Young Kara, with her drill-boring teenage intelligence, steals the show here. All told, an assured performance."
—Kirkus Reviews

# HOLE IN THE WATER

# Robert Kearney

FAWCETT CREST • NEW YORK

A Fawcett Crest Book
Published by The Ballantine Publishing Group
Copyright © 1997 by Robert Kearney

All of the characters in this book are fictitious, and any resemblance to actual persons, living or dead, is purely coincidental.

*BUT NOT FOR ME*, Music and lyrics by George Gershwin and Ira Gershwin. © 1930 (Renewed) WB Music Corp. All Rights Reserved. Used by permission. WARNER BROS. PUBLICATIONS U.S. INC., Miami, FL 33014.

http://www.randomhouse.com

Library of Congress Catalog Card Number: 97-97226

ISBN 0-449-00175-X

This edition published by arrangement with Doubleday, a division of Bantam Doubleday Dell Publishing Group, Inc.

Printed in Canada

First Ballantine Books Edition: August 1998

10  9  8  7  6  5  4  3  2  1

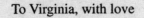

To Virginia, with love

Thanks to Mab Nulty, Virginia Kearney, Larry Sutin, Ginny Kelley, and Jonathan and Wendy Lazear for their encouragement and their many helpful suggestions. Special thanks to Marjorie Cox for her tenacious attention to detail. And my lifelong appreciation to the FPB writers, for letting me travel with them from Dinkytown to Warren's attic and beyond.

# One

The ferry swayed just as the old Subaru station wagon lurched over the ramp and pulled on board. Gretchen grabbed the armrest and swore, but strictly to herself. She did not even mouth the words. Her years as a teacher had taught her how to release her frustrations without inviting even more anarchy into her classroom.

Chuck braked the car abruptly, throwing her forward. This time the oath escaped—"Christ!"—but that was all. He killed the engine. Immediately, she could feel the uneven chugging of the diesels, the fluid pulse of a pump. An exhaust vent sputtered hoarsely, was buried under a heavy wave, then sputtered again.

She glanced over her shoulder at Kara, who was awake now but still huddled into the pillows, nestled against the door. Her daughter looked back, sleep-dulled and impassive, then closed her eyes. She shifted, and a thick lock of

1

hair—straight and golden, so unlike Gretchen's own dark
coppery curls—fell across her cheek. With her eyes still
closed, Kara tucked the loose hair behind her left ear, revealing three small gold hoops. When she was drowsy
like this, Kara's lips fell into a baby's pout. Gretchen
wanted to reach back and pat her, once, on the leg. Brush
a palm across the worn denim.

Beside Gretchen, Chuck's thin face rested on his fists
on the top arch of the steering wheel. His eyes were open,
staring blankly ahead. Sweat glistened in the dark twists
of his hair. He exhaled sharply, squeezed his eyes closed.
Silence, then a sudden sucking of air. She touched his
thigh. He didn't respond. Another suck of air.

"Are you OK? Can I get you something?"

He shook his head.

"Drink of water?"

"Are you kidding?"

He raised his pale eyelids, rolled down the window.
"It's twenty-one minutes across. I just have to sit very
quietly and not listen and not look at the water and think
about something else."

He had told her something about this. He'd explained
that the ferry ride would be a problem. She anticipated
some hesitation, some discomfort, but nothing like this.

The ferry's ramp grated against the cement pier and a
truck drove aboard, pulling into the space on Gretchen's
side of the car. The truck's exhaust mixed with the engine
fumes swirling within the ferry's high walls and the stench
of grease and oil-slicked harbor water. She was sure
Chuck was going to vomit.

A loose spray of raindrops splattered against the windshield and moved on.

Suddenly, Gretchen saw a khaki-shirted belly fill

Chuck's window. Three grimy fingers hooked over the edge, then four more. Slowly, the man bent down until a small, weathered face slid into view. Stark blue eyes set in a nest of wrinkles, sheltered from the rain by a dirty blue Zebco fishing cap. A large nose and a stubby beard.

"So, you came back." The voice was high-pitched but joyless and uninflected, the sound of a nail being clawed out of wood.

Chuck's eyes opened slowly. "Captain Gromek."

"Couldn't make it up here when he's sick, but when it comes time to pick over the bones . . ."

"That's out of line, Gromek."

The old man pinched his eyebrows—wispy patches of black, struck with coarse gray hairs. "Couldn't even come for the funeral. But a will reading . . . now that's a different kind of a deal, isn't it?"

"I said, that's out of line."

"So you did." Gromek stood, faced one way, then back. Gretchen thought he must be scanning the deck, monitoring the teenage boy who was directing the cars and trucks on board. He bent his face to the window again.

"Your father was a different man during the last year of his life. I don't know who or what he was at the end. But I know who you are. And who you were. And so does everyone else up here."

Chuck pounded once on the steering wheel, so that a sharp bleat erupted. "What am I supposed to do here? I'm forty-two years old. Am I supposed to get out of my car and punch you?"

"Not necessary."

"Well then, get out of my face. Get up in the pilot-house and get us to the island."

The old man stood in his shoes. "No one tells me what to do or where to go on my ship, mister." He straightened up, so that the sagging front of his khaki shirt filled the Subaru's window again. His right hand still rested on the edge, and Gretchen noticed that one of his fingers was missing, severed at the big knuckle.

After a moment, he bent over again. "All the other boys changed. Good or bad, they became different as they got older. But you, you haven't changed."

Chuck swore under his breath.

The high-pitched voice fell to a whisper: "People still know what you are." The old man shuffled back a step. For an instant, his eyes washed over Gretchen, then Kara. He did not acknowledge them. Instead, he turned and shambled away, between the cars, across the rain-beaten metal deck.

# Two

**2:00 P.M.**

The drive through northern Wisconsin had been pleasant but tiresome. First there had been square after square of not quite prosperous farms, bounded by windrows or plots of ramrod firs planted in perfect patterns like so much corn. The geometry was broken—here and there— by swatches of scrub and random pines and spruces; land that had once been farmed and now was not.

As they drove farther north, the unmanaged greenery became more common, then finally predominant. It looked like forest, and great lengths of it had been labeled as such by the Wisconsin DNR, but it didn't feel like forest to Gretchen. It wasn't dark or threatening or truly ancient. She guessed it was land that had fallen under the plow and then fallen back to nature. Men and women had ceased controlling it because it wasn't worth the effort. The land had won by wearing people out.

Then came Lake Superior. Her new husband had made the lake sound like a thing that was actively managed. Commercial fishing boats sailed around the Apostle Islands under a cloud of gulls, he'd said. Sport fishermen and charter sailors dotted the channels in the day and anchored in the bays during the cool night, shedding golden cabin light on the black water. In the winter, he'd explained to Kara, after the lake froze, they plowed the snow aside and drove cars from the mainland to Madeline Island.

"They take their old Christmas trees, and stake them out on the sides of the road to mark it," he'd said. "It's actually part of the U.S. highway system. The only stretch that disappears every summer." She imagined the trees, with shreds of tinsel still knotted in their boughs, shining in the January sun. Making something charming and functional out of old discards—sort of a municipal craft project. Overseen by winter-idled, civic-minded fishermen in red Hudson's Bay coats.

The specifics might or might not be true, but the impression—that this frigid heaving mass of ragged waves could be managed or overseen by humans—was a lie. She knew this as soon as they made the turn by the Seagull Motel at the edge of Bayfield and finally saw the lake, running out to a smear on the horizon. One-tenth of the world's fresh water.

"Nice trip to the beach," Kara had remarked, shivering.

"Kara, this is November in Wisconsin," Gretchen said. "You don't go swimming in Lake Superior in November. People in California don't go swimming in November." She wasn't sure of this, but she was sure enough to say it to her sixteen-year-old daughter. "You enjoy it on its own terms. It's a different sensibility."

Kara snorted.

Gretchen looked to Chuck for support, but he was not listening. They were still a half mile from the water, but the fear was already working on him. His eyes were fixed. His hands were rigid on the steering wheel. Gray complexion. She'd expected some kind of seasickness. Now she could see how bad it was and she worried that he wouldn't be able to reach the pier and negotiate the car onto the ferry.

He made it to the ferry. And he made the crossing without getting sick. But when they reached the island, he asked her to walk around the car and get in the driver's side. He wasn't going to drive for a little while.

She pulled off the ferry, following the vehicles ahead of her as they moved down the broad pier and across the cement apron, still in file, then into the small village. The line dispersed gradually—a mud-splattered pickup truck shooting off down a side street, a gray minivan pulling over beside the small store. Chuck was mostly silent, showing her with a hand signal or a few words to drive past the store, and the gas station, then to turn onto a quiet street that suddenly broadened into a highway.

She said nothing until the village of La Pointe, and the ferry ride, were a few miles behind them. "Was that . . . especially bad for you? I mean, was it worse because the water was so rough?"

He shook his head and didn't speak for a moment. Then: "It wasn't so rough."

"Hard to imagine what really bad weather would be like." She shook her head. "Is it bad for you . . . is it *as* bad for you, even when it's calm? Or was it, when you lived here?" She hesitated, felt flustered, unsure if she was asking too much. Or not enough. "Is this something you want to talk about?"

He took a long, wavering breath, let it out in a sigh. Another breath, less forceful. "It comes and goes. When I lived here I was more used to it. I think."

"This is a bad idea, isn't it?"

He nodded. "Probably."

"I hate this now," she said. "I don't want to feel like it's my fault we're doing this. You decided too."

"OK."

"OK, I pressured you," she admitted in a rush. "But you have certain rights here and you have to make sure they're protected. If you don't watch over your affairs, who will? Lawyers. After they got into your father's estate, there'd be nothing left."

"I suppose." The color was coming back into his face and he was massaging his hands. He's back, she thought. I wonder if it hurts to clench your fists that tightly.

They passed the town dump on the left, its shield of pines hiding the sight but not the smell of burning trash. "And who was that old guy? That captain?"

"Local hero."

"But what's his problem?"

"He hated my guts. Still hates them, apparently."

"Why?"

Chuck stretched out his thin legs. "Ancient history. His kid and I would get in trouble. Normal stuff, but the old man always blamed me. Then Donny went into the Marines. I didn't. Donny got blown up in a boiler explosion on a ship somewhere. Somehow that was my fault too." He rubbed his hands over his face. Suddenly, he looked pale again. "Ancient history," he repeated.

Most of his ancient history was a mystery to her.

They'd been together just short of a year. And she knew him even less than might be expected after that long. The night they'd met, at a party held by someone neither of them knew, they'd agreed that the greatest barrier to creating new intimacy was the reluctance to recount one's petty history again and again. "Look at people our age," he'd said. "They all marry friends, or each other's spouses, or people they've worked with for five years. They haven't got the heart to tell their stories from the beginning to strangers."

He'd slipped his hand under her elbow then, and gently tugged her out of the crowded kitchen into a hall. "I'd like to go out with you," he said, smiling shyly. "But I can't spend one more evening pushing tiger shrimp or some other date food around my plate while I tell a person I don't know very well what I was like in high school study hall." She smiled and extended her hand: deal. "Or my disastrous relationships," he went on, and when she pulled back her hand he stumbled over his words. "Well, OK, OK. That's obligatory, I suppose. But it's not something you leap into. Family and old lovers will come up. And I want to know about yours too. Eventually. For now, though, I'd like to spend some time with you. Just *see,* you know?"

She stuck out her hand again, and they discovered that they delighted each other in conversation, in bed, and playing tennis. He was respectful and affectionate toward her daughter. After seven months, they decided to get married. And they had, just two months ago, a few weeks after her divorce from Billy was finalized. By then, their previous lives had receded before their shared history. They each knew disjointed facts about the other, but those facts were never knit together. And Gretchen saw no reason to chase his dead past now.

Kara had fallen asleep on the ferry. When she gave a low groan, Gretchen spoke to her. "Hey, sweetie. Kara. We're almost there." She glanced at Chuck again, monitoring his complexion.

Gretchen's daughter fussed on the bench seat, pulling the oversized sweater closer around her neck.

"Kara?"

She pulled herself up abruptly, then slumped against the door. She flicked the long golden hair out of her face. "I have this unbelievable headache." Kara never whined anymore. Instead everything came out like this, perfectly deadpan, perfectly undifferentiated from anything else: "I have this unbelievable headache." "My tennis shoes are white." "A guy I know got his leg broken in a fight." At least, thought Gretchen, she'll never become a theater person.

Now she said, "I always get migraines from exhaust leaks."

"There is no exhaust leak and you don't have a migraine. Look outside. That's the lake." Gretchen couldn't see much of it, but the white foam peaks flashed by whenever there was a break in the trees.

"I think I know when I have a migraine."

"I think we will all have migraines if we keep this up just a little longer." The lake appeared suddenly, then hid again behind clumps of birch and maples clinging to their last scarlet and lemon-gold leaves.

Kara spoke, her jaw burrowed into the neck of her sweater: "It's pretty here."

"Yeah," Chuck said. "Even when I hated it, I had to admit it was beautiful."

"So you didn't hate it all the time." Kara let her inflection fall between asking and saying.

"Do you hate where you live all the time?" he asked. Gretchen glanced into the rearview mirror but couldn't see her daughter.

"Takes too much energy," Kara said flatly.

"Exactly." They rode in silence for a while and then he said, "It's a lot of work to actively hate something. Maybe you don't hate Thirty-sixth Avenue all the time, but it's still work to hate it as much as you do. Someday soon we're going to move, and you'll suddenly have all this energy. We'll have to get you a hobby or something. Teach you stenciling and have you redo all the rooms." His mouth arced into a faint smile.

Gretchen felt a rush of affection for him then, for not letting the weirdness keep a hold on him. For knowing how to kid her daughter. For not getting sick. For saying, again, in front of her and Kara, that he intended to take any money from his father's will and buy a house for them all. A house in a place where she didn't need to look at the unbarred basement windows and worry that they were a breach of security. Where they could walk out in the evening and forget to lock the doors or decide willfully to not lock the doors. Where her daughter could walk home from a friend's house after dark without her keys protruding between her fingers. Their safe house.

"All the rooms?" She mocked him. "Like we could afford a decent-sized house."

He shrugged. "Get a junker. Restore it. Could happen."

"Right."

"Hey, if I can fix up houses for other people, I can fix up one for myself. Get an old lady house, something that's been let go. Do something with the woodwork, retile the bathrooms, sand the floors. Rip out the kitchen linoleum and put in a nice little parquet or some ceramic."

"Right."

Gretchen winced for him. Kara was only teasing, but this was cruel territory. She wanted to stop her but knew it would be more belittling to him than the teasing.

"OK, maybe it won't happen. But if Leo didn't take another mortgage on the house . . . and if he decided to leave it to me . . . then it's got to be worth something. It's got over a hundred feet of shoreline. We sell it, and buy something for ourselves. That's what you call *home free*."

He's OK, Gretchen thought. Solid when solid was needed. Bullheaded from decades of being on his own, but not pushy. They fought now and then, and he was not especially good at finishing up with his anger and getting rid of it. But he was not going to leave them. He was not going to go out for a pack of Vantages and then call a week later from Boulder, quoting Bruce Springsteen.

Chuck had already bummed around in Boulder. And Berlin. And La Paz before the drugs, and Kabul before the war. Now he said he wanted money in the bank and a home. And family—he swore his gratitude to her for bringing Kara into his life when he was not likely to start a family of his own. He said he wanted to provide for them, a preposterously retro gender role, especially since she had been providing for herself and Kara—not well but well enough—on her teacher's salary. But she found it charming that he would say such things, and expedient that he meant them. She wanted to buy a house someplace nice.

His edginess and pallor seemed to come in waves, but the peaks and troughs became gentler as they drove.

"This cinder-block building that looks like a welding shop—that's where Leo used to preach."

"Really? I assumed the little church in La Pointe . . ."

Chuck grunted. "That is a den of liberal Congregationalists. Leo wouldn't walk on that side of the street. He bullied the locals so no one would go there. Back when I left people were calling it the Tourist Church."

She smiled and he went on, pointing out the stone-and-timber lodge his grandparents owned when they first brought his mother to the island. The house Leo had been born in. The cabin his friend Art had bought when he came back from the service, an old hunting lodge with no plumbing but the best natural anchorage on the island. "He still lives there, I heard. Fixed it up a little, I hope."

He turned back to Kara. "Every wall inside Art's house was dark green. There'd been a train wreck just outside of Bayfield and a boxcar of paint had popped off the tracks. People got there right away and started grabbing gallons, carrying them into the woods and hiding them. For years after, everyone had green walls and green basement floors. All the kids had green forts in their backyards. People started calling the color Trainwreck Green."

He was still describing the bachelor squalor of Art's place when they crested a small hill. "That house with the antenna on it is the sheriff's place," he said. "You see that little outbuilding there? That's Trainwreck Green. You'd think he might have repainted it in thirty years."

He stared at the house as he passed. "We don't have police on the island," he said absently. "We have a deputy sheriff, which is convenient because it's the highest authority recognized by your mainline survivalist fanatics."

For the next ten minutes he told them about the politics

of the island, and how his father had been at the center of it: "He was very good at pushing the limits with the government, so the locals rallied around him. But he always knew when to stop. He was audited by the IRS year after year, but they never found anything. He was in court all the time with them, filing motions and contesting whatever . . . a real hayseed litigator. The state attorneys . . ."

The car slipped around an evergreen-lined curve and his voice quickly trailed off. "There it is," he said. She slowed without thinking, then pushed down again on the accelerator. Ahead, a huge, weathered gray clapboard house perched on the hill above the pounding lake.

"Nothing's changed," he said.

She pulled onto the thin scatter of gravel that stood for a driveway, cut the engine, and stepped out.

# Three

Chuck edged out of the car. Pine needles littered the walkway, collected in the cracks in the cement. He slipped the key into the lock, awkwardly, then realized that the old green door was not locked after all. He leaned into it; the door stuck at first, swollen with the moisture in the air, then swung in quickly.

Inside, little had changed in twenty years. To his left, the same sun-faded blue rag rug lay on the floor under the same white table. An unironed tablecloth, white with small green flowers, was spread over it. The living room with its wood stove was on his right. He knew that some of the furniture must have been changed, but everything looked familiar: the worn plaid couch, the wingback chair. Next to the stove, the high wooden chair—almost a throne—with lion's claws for feet: Leo's chair, where he would have his nightly glass of whiskey. Behind it,

15

through the sliding doors, was the deck overlooking the water, where Leo had spent many hours sleeping and eating and reading. Beyond that, the rocky beach. Then the water.

Everything seemed immediately and oppressively drab to him. He turned to apologize.

"Oh, Chuck," his wife said, "it's absolutely splendid. It's so *big*. And all the light. It must be blinding on a sunny day." She moved eagerly about the rooms, touching things, glancing up the stairs, and he hated her for not feeling the dreary weight.

"Can we go outside?" she asked, and he nodded toward the kitchen and the side door. They filed out, Kara shuffling behind them. Directly across from the open back door was the storage shed. Ever since he'd been in junior high school, it had been leaning away from the lake and to the north, against a tree. Between it and the house, a long flight of unpainted stairs led down to the lake. Gretchen started down.

"What's that?" Kara asked, nodding toward the shed.

"The proverbial woodshed, my dear," he said. He wandered toward it.

"Did your dad actually knock you around in there?"

"Leo never saw any need to bring his discipline away from the comfort of the living room. But it was a place for punishment. He used to load this thing up with wood in the summer and fall, and it was my job to split it for the winter." He pushed his foot against the base of the door, and it swung open. The rich smell of a decaying building filled his nostrils.

For all the shed's external collapse, the interior had been maintained. Paint had been applied to the window frames. The firewood was gone—stacked outside now, he'd noticed—and the floor had been swept. Now the shed was filled with cast-off furniture and equipment, neatly stacked along the north and west walls. Leo had even wired it: a long cord stretched down from the rafters, with a single lightbulb at the end.

He turned to leave but, looking over his shoulder, he saw something else. It was propped up against the wall in the back corner, behind a broken-down recliner, under an old machine-quilted bedspread. He peeled back a corner, smiled at the sky-blue metal, then peeled back more. His Triumph.

"Cool motorcycle." Kara, silhouetted in the door, made a clicking sound. "Was it yours?" She stepped closer now to inspect it.

"Yes and no. Leo bought it for me when I was sixteen. He'd had one as a boy and thought I should have one too." He smiled at her, then pulled off the rest of the quilt. "I hated it. Every time I got on it, I thought I was going to go out of control and slide across the road into a passing truck. Have my head crushed like a watermelon. Sort of a personal phobia."

"You mean you had this great bike and never got into it?" She snorted. "Wuss."

"Thank you." He bent over to inspect the engine, noting that Leo had been maintaining it. New spark plugs, no rust or caked-on grease. Not even any cobwebs. "I got to know the mechanics well enough," he went on. "That's how I managed to keep from having to ride it. I just kept working on the damn thing, so it was never really put together."

"And since then it's just been sitting here?" She sighed. "It's so cool."

"Maybe we should bring it home with us?"

He regretted teasing her as soon as he saw the wild joy in her face. She looked at him then and saw that he wasn't serious and the joy soured.

"You're too young," he said quickly. "I couldn't teach you how to ride it."

"I already know how."

"You do? Where did you learn how to ride a bike?"

She cocked her head at him. "I do have a life. And you and Mom don't know *everything* about it."

He cocked his head back at her. "Aren't we supposed to?"

"Good luck." She gave the bike a last look. "I'm going down to the lake to find Mom. And when you tell on me, tell her I learned from Kenny." She turned abruptly and walked out. She was a master of the truncated conversation, the hairpin shift. It seemed rude when you first met her, and time didn't soften that impression.

He re-covered the old bike and stepped out of the shed, suddenly aware of how rancid the air had been inside. The stiff breeze blowing in off the lake was stripped of decay, stripped of contamination, the pure scent of air that had rubbed up against the black of space.

Below, his wife and daughter were walking out across the old pier. Now a battered finger of stone and concrete, the pier was a tribute to the three horns of backwoods engineering: pigheaded resolve, slipshod workmanship, and insufficient funds. Leo had hired one of his goofball politico buddies—old Bone Torkson—to construct the pier on a budget because Torkson needed work and because Leo thought that it might serve a purpose.

Whatever the purpose, he had never made it clear to his young son. At one point Leo called it a fishing dock. At another, he said it would be useful if he ever wanted to keep a sailboat at the house. Once he said the best thing would be to put a bench at the end, where he could sit in the evening, away from the mosquitoes, and smoke a pipe.

Torkson appeared every morning for five weeks, wearing faded coveralls, a yellowed thermal undershirt showing at the neck, his waders thrown over a shoulder, lunch sack in hand. He was a small man but so sinewy and tough that someone had once compared him to a rawhide dog toy. The image stuck, and from then on he was known as Bone.

He was a friend of Leo's, but Bone Torkson never came inside while he was working on the pier. And Leo never offered to help move the big rocks that served as the pier's foundation, or push the wheelbarrows of concrete. He would stand at the kitchen window, arms crossed so that the old flannel shirt stretched across his muscled back, watching Torkson work. Chuck thought the new formality was a way to keep the project on a professional footing, prevent it from seeming like charity.

If Torkson had hoped to earn self-respect as well as an income, he wound up short. He tried to save money on the project by stretching the concrete until it was a chalky soup. Within a year or so, the pier was crumbling away and soon the thing became an eyesore: a jumble of rocks and shattered concrete that caught and held all manner of lake-borne garbage, from fishing line to waterlogged trees to plastic bags.

Gretchen and Kara were standing about five feet from the end, letting the wave spume flirt with their shoes. They looked perfect from this vantage: the mother cautious but assured, making graceful leaps on thin legs; her teenage daughter reckless, bounding over wave-slicked rocks on thighs muscled by years of soccer, whooping at modest dangers.

He wanted to go join them, but could not.

The wind picked up and freshened the light drizzle. Slowly, Gretchen and Kara made their way back to the beach and up the stairs to the shed.

He watched his wife mount the stairs, her wind-rouged cheeks creased with a broad smile. She had turned forty a month before. Several of her friends had said she seemed much younger, but they were lying. As far as he could tell, she seemed exactly her age: handsome, often pretty, but not a ravishing youth. He suspected she never had been. She had the kind of good looks that might be overlooked in a younger woman, but became more attractive—even seductive—with age.

When she reached him on the landing, his wife slipped her slender arm under his and around his waist, and applied just enough pressure to show she thought the house and the beach were grand. A cold disgust swept through him; she was going to suggest they not sell the house. That they keep it for vacations.

That will change, he thought. Soon enough she'll understand and then she'll never want to see this place again. She'll beg me to sell it. And she'll never look back.

"Can we go inside now?" Kara said. "I'm freezing."

They entered by the side door, into the kitchen. Kara went first, and he held the door for Gretchen, looking past her as she entered, and then entered himself, head down. He looked up and glimpsed the looming shadow staggering from the dark hallway just as Kara screamed.

The shadow howled back at her and Kara dropped down, one hand instinctively rising, the other flicking long wet hair out of her face. "Mother!" she cried.

The shadow staggered forward again, this time into the kitchen light, and in an instant he knew it was Mrs. Ford. She was carrying a wicker basket of laundry in her knobby hands. "Who the hell are . . ." She started to howl again but caught sight of Chuck and stopped. Her mouth yapped noiselessly, twice, and finally the words came out. "You. Chuck. Oh, my God."

Kara was already smiling wildly, shaking off the spasm of fear, her hand on her chest. "Whew!"

The old woman put her basket, piled with sheets, on the kitchen table. Her hair was still gray and tied up in back, the dress still her trademarked plain cotton plaid, the shoes black and clunky. But her eyes were a raw, honeyed red. And she had gained weight, a lot of it, so that her body seemed to sag around her bones now, and her face was thick and jowly and ashen. He could see that even in the afternoon's dreary light: her color was bad.

"Hi, Mrs. Ford. Sorry to have given you a scare." He introduced Gretchen and Kara, then added, "Mrs. Ford has been coming in to cook and clean for my father for many, many years."

"You couldn't tell a person you were coming, I suppose. You could have given me a stroke."

"We tried to call a couple of times but couldn't reach you. I sent a letter too. You didn't get it?"

"No letters at all," she said. Her lips quickly curved down. Her raw eyes dulled. "Or maybe I got them and didn't open them. But someone could have said something to me." She closed her eyes a moment and sighed.

"I was told you were there, with Leo," he said. "I'm sure it meant an awful lot to him."

She shrugged. "Cancer of the pancreas steals up on people," she said. "They are fine and then they die. It's real quick. That's the blessing of it, I guess. It's painful but quick." Her knobby hands relaxed on the wicker basket, then bunched again. "Even with the pain, he kept his dignity all through it. I thought you would like to know that. He was as strong in death as he was in life." She turned toward Gretchen. "Not everyone is. My sister, lying on her deathbed, made little noises. Little sharp screaming noises. For over an hour."

"And you've been all right?" Chuck asked quickly.

"It's amazing how much I know about various kinds of cancer," she went on. "Forty, fifty years ago, people didn't follow it so closely, I guess. Now it seems like it's all people talk about."

"I'm very sorry for you, Mrs. Ford."

"And I for you all." She stared abruptly at Kara, then swung her attention to Gretchen. "You'll want to stay here tonight, I suppose."

"If we could . . ." Gretchen began. "Well, actually, I guess, yes. Assuming . . . Is the house . . . livable? I mean, it's OK and everything?"

"Yeah, sure. I'll make up the beds as soon as these sheets are dry." She patted the laundry in the basket.

He wondered who had dirtied the sheets. It had been over a month since his father died. "No rush," he said. "We have to go into town for the will reading later this afternoon. I assume you're going too?"

"Pick over the bones? No, sir. Wilkerson told me to come but I don't want to be around when everyone gets to fighting over who got what. I can't think of anything more disgusting."

He felt the acid rinse his stomach. "What do you mean 'everyone'?"

"Wilkerson didn't tell you?" She bent over the basket

but made no move to lift it. "Leo's whole congregation is invited. The whole crazy bunch of them. You know some of the church money was lost."

"No . . ."

"Well, after that, he felt he owed it to them to show that he hadn't been hiding anything. That it really was gone." She stared at Kara again, as if puzzled by her presence. "I'm afraid there's not much in the fridge at the moment."

"That's fine," he said. "We brought food with us. I didn't know that you were still . . ."

"Oh, yes. Of course." She was shuffling now, caught between her roles as housekeeper and host. Then it struck him.

"Excuse me, Mrs. Ford. This is sort of confusing for all of us, I know. But . . . were you living here? I mean, are you living here now? It's OK . . ."

Her voice hardened. "And what is that supposed to mean?"

"It doesn't mean anything. It was a question."

"I will not take any smart remarks from you. And I will not take any snide suggestions." Here she pointed her finger, a thing of thick, blanched flesh. "And don't think you can frighten me."

"Look. Forget I asked," he said. "Forget it."

"Not on your life," said Mrs. Ford. She hefted the laundry off the table. "I'd hoped to hang these sheets on the deck. But it's drizzling, if you haven't noticed."

# Four

The Subaru had a gas smell if you sat in the back seat.
You couldn't smell it in the front seat, and her mother
and Chuck never sat in the back, so they didn't realize it.
She thought about insisting that one of them sit there, just
to prove her point, but never did. Never complain, never
explain, never let them see you sweat. Take a lot of
Tylenol.

Tylenol was her friend. Cure for cheap wine and loud
music. Cramps and gas fumes. Actually not that good for
cramps and gas fumes, but it was what she carried. But
maybe she wouldn't be carrying it that much longer, because she was pretty much sick of bad wine and sloppy
loud guitar riffs. She'd spent too much time in Gordo's
basement in the past six months. The whole freaking
summer, it seemed. Headaches and clumsy lust. Time to
ditch all that and the Tylenol too.

She was so sick of Gordo's basement she didn't mind spending Thanksgiving vacation with her mother and Chuck, even up on the tundra or whatever this was. OK, she minded. Her head was pounding. She wished she were home. Home, and ten pounds thinner, and with friends who were not grotesque and who liked her the way she was.

She cracked the Subaru's window even though it was drizzling. Chuck wouldn't say anything because he was either too spaced or didn't care. He was detached in a way that was very weird and very dull at the same time. Her mother was spaced a lot too, but she never, never didn't care. She had something to say about everything. All the time.

"Aren't you cold back there, honey?" she asked.

"No. I wanted some air."

"Still have your headache?"

"No, I'm OK." My brain is swelling. Leeches are eating my butt flesh. Leave me alone.

Chuck drove through the four corners that was the village and pulled over in front of a small store. He spoke to her mother, then over his shoulder to her. "Want anything?" She shook her head. "Pop, snacks, anything?" She shook again.

He zipped up his brown leather jacket, opened the car door, leaped out, sprinted toward the store, stopped midway, sprinted back, rapped on her mother's window even as she was lowering it. "Money. Money. You've got the money in your purse." Her mother opened her purse, dug out her wallet and a twenty-dollar bill, and he muttered at her the whole time, saying, "Come on. Come on. It's raining out here." While he muttered, he danced on the curb, hopping from one foot to the other, as though he could dodge the drops. This was his other weird side: he could be impassive and silly and the next minute turn hyper and short-tempered.

With the money in hand, he jogged back through the drizzle, snarling at the rain, his black hair bobbing around his head. Sometimes his upper lip seemed to pull up, as if he were snarling, even when he wasn't. She thought it had something to do with his nose, but she wasn't sure what. Now he *was* snarling—at the rain or this island or the prospect of his father's will reading with everyone else from the island there, listening.

He slipped behind a screen door. From the signs outside and what she could see through the windows, the screen door was the common entrance to a small grocery store (on the left), a bar (off to the right), and a restaurant (which she guessed was straight down the hall).

Kara hesitated, then quickly opened her purse. "Actually . . . ," she began. She rummaged up the eleven quarters she would need. "You want anything, Mom?"

"No, and neither do you."

"Mom. Come on." She pushed down on the door handle. "I changed my mind. I just want a Coke or something. You sure you're OK?"

"You are not to buy cigarettes."

"Just a Coke. OK?"

"You have asthma, Kara."

"OK!" This would be my body, I believe. She ducked out, into the rain.

An instant later she was behind the screen door, looking into the minuscule convenience store—three aisles, lots of canned goods and trash foods and a freezer filled with the Fudgsicles left from the tourist season. Chuck was standing by a display near the back.

Straight down the hall, about fifteen feet from her, a pair of potted trees crowded the restaurant entrance. Just past the trees was a cash register and, beyond that, a few tables with blue-checkered tablecloths and, behind them, she could see through the window the slate-gray lake.

The bar's heavy door was propped open with a red-vinyl-upholstered stool. Inside it was dark, and loud with menacing laughter, but along the far wall she could see the hard red beacon of the cigarette machine. The laughter built again, and someone was pounding on the bar. She hesitated, glanced over her shoulder, and saw Chuck carrying his purchases toward the front counter of the store.

She ducked past the stool and skirted the crowd, which was gathered around something in the center of the room near the bar. Quickly, she thrust her quarters into the machine, but the last one fell through, rattling in the curved metal trough at the bottom. She tried it again. It clicked and jangled and fell out again.

A voice spoke close to her ear. "You need to put a little backspin on it." A tall, brown-haired man about Chuck's age leaned in, gave her a serious wink. "Heh-here," he stammered. "Give it to Brian." His eyebrows climbed in three jerks, then fell to rest. "Give it to the spin doctor." He plugged the last quarter with a downward stroke of his index finger, and it caught in the works. She pulled the silver knob below the Vantage pack and it tumbled softly out of the machine's guts.

When she nodded to him, he raised his can in an abrupt toasting motion, and a small wave of beer burbled out of the top and onto his hand.

"Drink much?" she asked.

"Too much, maybe." His watery eyes glistened in the machine's ruby light.

"Remember, save those pop-tops for the Ronald Mc-Donald houses."

He nodded nervously, twice, and grinned at her.

A roar arose behind her. "What's going on," she asked. Her eyes had adjusted by now and she could see that most of the patrons were standing in a circle.

"It's sad," Brian said.

She took a step forward and could now see a golden retriever in the center of the circle. The dog was drinking, lapping with slow persistence at a foamy bowl. A greasy bandanna, tied around its neck, drooped into the bowl beside its flicking tongue. A tall, stocky man, his face sheathed with a heavy red-brown beard, was adding beer from a bottle.

The dog stopped for a moment and the red-bearded man pushed the bowl across the room with his boot. He lifted his head and smiled, the neon lights glinting off thick aviator glasses. The dog followed, its head bowed, its legs stiff and wobbly. The crowd cheered.

Behind the bar, a nervous red-lipped little blonde woman watched. Her fake eyelashes blinked and her tiny stark mouth twitched. Now it was a broad grimace over clamped teeth; now her lips were pursed in sympathy. At one point it looked as though she was talking, but Kara couldn't hear any words coming out. The woman stuck her plump arm out over the bar to the bearded man with the aviator glasses but couldn't reach him. Didn't really try. The man ignored her—if he knew she was there—and pushed the beer bowl a few feet farther from the retriever. The dog staggered after it a step, then stopped, and lay down with its head on its paws.

"Ahh, she's done in," he said. "Overdid it again, eh, Maggie." He pushed the bowl back toward her and sighed theatrically. "Poor old girl, you aren't the same anymore." He patted her head. "Used to be you were the last one standing."

Kara stared mutely at the crowd before her. She had come in on the last act. Whatever had preceded, whatever was the degrading heart of the exhibition, it had passed. Now the poor dog was being patted and people were turning away. Still she pushed her way into the center of the room. "What is this?" She knelt next to the dog, which looked up at her with rheumy eyes. "It's beer. It's really beer." She stood, shook her head involuntarily, gave the bowl a furious kick. The dog cowered. Beer sprayed over the shoes of several men near the bar. Someone swore and kicked the bowl back at her but she didn't flinch. "You jerks!" she yelled. "I can't believe this." She moved toward the dog, but it whined and re- treated against the stools.

The bearded man grabbed her under the arm and pulled her up roughly. "My dog," he said. "Who the hell are you to mess around with my dog?"

Kara was frightened but her anger made her wild. "*You* made *your* dog an alcoholic. Let go of me." She broke free but the man came after her again.

"Leave her, Bartok," the bartender whinnied. "Leave her alone. She's a kid."

"Shut up, Jeanine."

Brian stepped forward and opened his mouth, stam- mering, "Ba-ba-ba."

"And I don't need a fucking idiot to tell me what to do, either."

"Hey, Bartok. Let her alone." This was another man's

voice, Chuck's, and Bartok looked up abruptly. He stopped and passed his eyes over her mother's husband, who stood in the doorway with a small brown bag under his arm.

"Well, shit. Look what the rain brought up."

Chuck said, "Come on, Kara."

"Oh, that's just *perfect*," Bartok said. "Two head cases." Kara walked around him toward Chuck and the crowd parted to let her through. "Is this sorry fuck your date, honey?"

"That's enough, Bartok."

A mocking "Ooooooo" rose up from the crowd.

"It's *what*?" Bartok moved toward them now, his hands balled at his sides. Behind him, someone yelled, "Freak," and someone else chanted, "Waterboy, Waterboy."

The red-lipped woman ducked her squat frame under the counter at the end of the bar and ran between them. "OK, keep it down now. I've had it with you all."

Bartok stood over her, in front of Chuck now. "This isn't your business, Jeanine."

"Art!" she yelled. "Art, you back there?"

Bartok smiled cruelly and said, "Normally, at a moment like this, I take off my glasses. In this case, I don't think I need to bother."

Kara pushed Chuck, trying to edge him out the door. She was nervous and it made her need to breathe harder and that made her uncomfortable. "Chuck. Let's go." Above her head, she felt Bartok's arm swing out, landing squarely on Chuck's shoulder, rocking him back against the jukebox.

"What about that, Waterboy? Come here. I'll give you a free shot." He spread his arms apart. "Let me have it. Or don't you want to fight?"

From the back of the bar, a voice rose up: "God damn it, Bartok. Why is it *always* you?" A stout man, hair still sun-bleached from the summer, worked his way toward them, muttering and fending off the light pushes he got from the other patrons. "OK, OK, what the hell's the deal here now?" As he came close to them, he slowed. "Christ on a stick. Chuck."

"Hi, Art." He never took his eyes off Bartok.

"What's the problem here, Bartok?"

"No problem. Little girl here came in, started raising hell, knocking beer all over the place." He glanced at Art. "Does she look twenty-one to you? Hell, I doubt if she's sixteen. You'd think Waterboy would have more pride than to come in here with this butt-ugly jailbait."

The blond man stared blankly at him. "Jesus, Bartok, that's so feeble. You're trying to pick a fight and that's the best you can do?"

"I already hit him once."

"Pathetic."

"Suppose I called her an eel pussy?"

Brian shuffled forward and in the same instant Chuck lunged at Bartok. Art slipped between them, his forearms landing squarely on Chuck's chest. Another blow from Bartok went around Art, glanced off Chuck's arm.

Art yelled as he pushed the two men apart, "OK. OK." He swung around to Bartok. "Shut the fuck up, Bartok. And your dog is eighty-sixed. Get her out of here. Brian, go find somewhere else to go for a while. And you two"—he turned to Chuck and Kara—"are outta here as well. Let's go."

He ushered them out the door and onto the street. "You OK?" he asked, and Kara thought he was talking to

Chuck. But when she looked up she could see that he was staring at her.

"They were feeding beer to that dog," she said. "That's got to be against the law."

"We've kicked Maggie out three or four times over the past year, but she keeps sneaking back in. It probably is against the law, now that you mention it. Cruelty to animals." He stood close to her, speaking directly to her, so serious that she was convinced he was mocking her. She was waiting for some stupid punch line but Art just nodded.

"You back to look after your dad's things?" Now he was talking to Chuck. "Sorry about his dying and all."

"Right," Chuck countered. They approached the Subaru. "He came down on you even more than on me. Hey, this is my wife's daughter, Kara. And here is my wife."

"No kidding."

Gretchen rolled down the window of the car and smiled.

"Gretchen, this is Art Sannar, a friend from my murky past. Just saved me from getting my tail kicked, just like the bad old days."

"Rock fever," Art said. "When it's bad weather like this, people get stuck on the island. If some of them don't get over to the mainland pretty soon, we're gonna see some real weird shit. Cannibalism and politics. You people staying long?"

"Just a couple of days, I guess," Gretchen replied.

"A couple of days! You're gone twenty years and that's it?" He shook his head at Chuck. "So what are you doing? You got a job?" He bent down to Gretchen. "The three most-asked questions around here: Got a job? What're you driving? When you gonna get your boat back in the water?" He laughed loudly and turned back to Chuck.

"I'm in remodeling," Chuck said. "Some carpentry, mostly tile work. Custom bathrooms, kitchens. Like that. Design. Installation. Whatever pays."

"No kidding." Again to Gretchen, he said, "He was always doing designs and things when we were younger. We'd get piles of rocks off the beach and he'd make these incredible mosaics. Birds, Indians . . . I remember this incredible . . . was it Hendrix?"

Chuck pointed a finger at Kara. "Yes, I did a sort of Peter Max mosaic of Jimi Hendrix and no one better laugh about it."

Kara put her hand over her mouth.

A gust of wind swept over them and the rain picked up. Chuck said, "Hop in, Kara." He began to walk around the car but stopped by the front. The two men spoke softly for a moment, their backs toward the car.

Her mother turned to her. "You OK? What happened?"

"Nothing you haven't seen in a Fellini movie."

"A Fellini movie. You've never seen a Fellini movie."

"Well, I know what they're about."

Her mother turned back in her seat. "You're the only one."

"These jerks were feeding beer to a dog and a guy tried to pick a fight with Chuck."

"Oh, God. Where are we?" Her mother shook her head. "This is such a bad idea."

In her calm, uninflected voice, Kara went on. "The guy said—and these were his words—said I was butt-ugly jailbait. And an eel pussy."

"*What?*"

A laugh escaped Kara. "You know, it's educational. You think you've been insulted in every conceivable way, and then, whoa! A new map to the land of degradation."

The rain picked up again, blurring the windshield, but neither man moved. Art was motioning now, and Gretchen could hear his laughter over the rain's faint drumming on the car roof. Past them, the screen door opened. Brian stepped out, stared vacantly up and down the street. Jeanine the bartender came behind him, moving just halfway out the door. She didn't wave to Chuck or Art. She just stood there, letting them see her watch them. Even at this distance, Kara could see the heavy eyelashes, which seemed clumped together with tears or rain or a fresh larding of mascara.

Finally, the two men moved apart. Chuck waved once to Art, put his hand on the car door, then saw Jeanine open the door another six inches. She stepped out into the rain but didn't come forward toward him. The light was fading quickly now under the heavy clouds. La Pointe's two streetlamps flickered on.

He let go of the car door, flipped his jacket collar over his neck, and walked over to her. She crossed her arms. He punched his hands deep into his jacket pockets. Brian stood over them, turning his head slowly from Chuck to Jeanine as they talked. Chuck touched Brian on the elbow, then jogged back to the car.

"This bites," Chuck said. He shook the rain off his coat collar, brushed it out of his hair. "This whole thing really bites. Don't be surprised if we walk away from this reading with something less than we have now."

"That's impossible," her mother said.

Chuck didn't say anything. He stared at Gretchen for a

long time. And Kara stared at Chuck for so long that he started to look like a hook-beaked bird. Or a small, sharp-faced mammal. A mink, maybe. Thinking it—seeing it so clearly—made her embarrassed and she twisted her eyes away.

# Gromek

*If someone had told me forty years ago that some feelings
didn't fade out, I would have believed him. But if he'd
told me that there are feelings that come back to you as
bright and fresh as the paint on a new car, I would have
laughed out loud.*

*I was a drunk forty years ago, and a lot of my life—
feelings, thoughts, yearnings—faded away. And quick.
But now I can remember so many feelings so well. I have
always thought of myself as an emotional man, so perhaps I'm more inclined this way than some others. I don't
think so, though. Every man I know is emotional. Why
else would they do what they do? Why would they marry?
Work like a damn mule in some factory or on a boat?
Take care of their children and wife? Go to war? Come
home and try to start a normal life again?*

*I can't remember my feelings on the day my son was
born, except a kind of deep excitement. I cannot remember my feelings on the day I heard he died, or the day my*

*wife passed on, except that both days were filled with a sort of shapeless grief. It was a deep emotion, but today I can't really recall what it felt like.*

*I do recall my emotions the day I caught my hand in a winch and ripped out one of my fingers. It's easy to recall because there was a shape to that: I knew that I would not be doing some things again, at least not in the easy ways that I had been doing them. And I knew I was grateful to Leo, because he was the one that kept me from losing more fingers, my hand, my arm.*

*Strange, but I can remember my sadness when I first needed to get bifocals, even though I wasn't a young man. I can recall the fear I've felt a hundred times on the lake. The shame I've felt lately, because I've been too proud to give over command of my ship when I was not fit to command her because of drink or fatigue. You can run a million gallons of crude oil into the waters off Alaska and be the world's villain, but imagine how much worse it would feel to lose a human life? Pull a living thing out of someone's family. And still I can't stop myself.*

*I recall the sadness I felt when I stopped trusting Leo, and my confusion when I kept giving him my money. I can't make sense of this, but I can recall it.*

*As soon as I saw him again, I recalled how bright and fresh my hatred was for Leo's boy. I don't try to justify it. But it came to me with the force of something larger than the hate one person feels for another. This also had to do with the love one feels for one's country, one's flag. I do not recognize the authority of this country to do certain things, but I do love her. And I would fight to defend her. And I expect the same of all her sons.*

*I can't forgive him and I don't want to anyway. You could say this is harsh and I don't deny it, but it is a true*

*and deep emotion. I'll never forgive him. It doesn't mat-*
*ter to me whether he was just acting or truly crazy. What*
*he has done throughout his life—to himself, his animals,*
*his wife, his father—is unforgivable. I don't know for a*
*fact that he'll face justice in this life for what he did, but I*
*feel that he will. After all these years, I still feel it.*

# Five

**4:00 P.M.**

Chuck wanted to sit in the car and collect himself, not talking or even thinking, but they kept looking at him and their breathing, with the drizzle and humidity, made the windshield fog up and weighted the air. It was hard to inhale. Hard to get that cleansing wash of fresh air. He rolled down the window and let the rain splatter against his face.

"You OK?" she asked.

It took a few seconds and he felt better.

"Yeah," he said. He rolled up the window, turned the key in the ignition.

She folded back his jacket collar, flicked a few droplets of rain off his hair. "What happened in there?"

"No big deal," he said.

"Kara said they were forcing a dog to drink beer. And someone called her jailbait?"

"Something like that. Kara yelled at them and they yelled at her and then I came in. And they yelled at me."

He steered the station wagon out of town, south this time, toward the lawyer's house. "Kara did the right thing."

"I kicked beer on them," she said.

"That was maybe unnecessary," Chuck said. "These are not the kind of people you want to piss off. But just so you know—the jailbait part was directed at me more than you. He was just trying to get to me. Some of these people started riding my tail twenty or thirty years ago."

"So were you like the most despised person on this island?"

"Kara!" Gretchen scolded her but he laughed.

"Well, jeez," Kara said. "The boat captain hates you and Mrs. Ford hates you and your dad hated you and those guys in the bar hate you . . ." She was giggling and he laughed with her.

"You got it," he said.

"What'd you do?"

"Lots of wicked things."

"Were you the rebel of Madeline Island?" He nodded and she leaned forward, between the front seats, the better to needle him. "You were the bad boy of the island even though you lived with your dad? And were afraid to ride your motorcycle? And you were terrified of the water?"

"A life lesson there, sweetheart. You can be a rebel *and* a complete simp." He smiled back at her and thought: What the hell. As good a time as any. "I was just normally despised until I was seventeen. Then I was institutionalized for a while and they got serious about it." He drove a hundred yards in silence, waiting for one of them to speak. When neither of them did, he pulled the car over, the crush of gravel suddenly loud.

He spoke to Kara in the rearview mirror. He didn't want to look at Gretchen just yet.

"When I was around your age, guys had basically two choices. They finished high school and went on to college, or they turned eighteen and got drafted and went to Vietnam. I wasn't college material in those days. But I wasn't going to go to Vietnam.

"I decided to beat the draft, but I didn't think I could do it on the usual physical stuff like weight or blood pressure. I went for a psychological exemption. And got it. I was pretty smart about it because I started setting things up early, when I was still seventeen. But I was so convincing that I got to spend about two months in a psychiatric hospital."

Gretchen said, "I thought people could just go to the right psychiatrist and get a schizophrenia diagnosis for two hundred dollars."

"In Minneapolis, maybe. Up here, we didn't have much of an underground. I had to do it all by myself."

"I never understood this," Kara said. "Couldn't you just say you were gay? And that was it?"

"Yep, but that was a much bigger deal than now. If there was another Nam on today, half the guys in America would be shopping in Victoria's Secret for something to wear to their draft physical. In those days, it was too humiliating. I can't explain it. Except to tell you that even guys who were legitimately gay decided to go to war rather than come out. I know one guy who did come out at his physical. The movement people . . ."

"The *movement people*?" Kara asked.

"As they were called. Anyway, they told him to write

up a letter, explaining that he was gay. He mentioned that he was going to use a typewriter at work, and they told him to destroy the typewriter ribbon afterward if he wanted to keep his job. That's a true story."

He glanced at his watch and put the car in gear. "We're gonna miss the will if we don't hurry."

Gretchen winced. "So? What did you do? To convince people."

"Un-uh." He shook his head.

He knew she wanted to push him, make him tell more. He could tell she was worried that some of it might be upsetting for Kara, but her curiosity was strong enough to overcome her maternal impulses. Before she could decide how to get what she wanted from him, Kara cut in: "Did people hate you more because they thought you were insane or because they thought you were a draft dodger?"

"I don't think many of them were that precise about it. Either way, they could find me repellent. They also hated me because I wasn't ashamed of not going over. There was all this tough talk and swaggering but in the end these guys were going off to war because their moms and dads said they had to. Or the government said so. All the tough guys fell in line and did what they were told. I didn't—and they didn't care if it was because I was crazy or because I was sane. I didn't say much about it but everyone knew I was proud of not going. It really pissed them off. Especially after people started coming home in body bags.

"The bitch of it was that they were pissed off about kids dying but they kept sending them over. And guys kept going. Guys came back from Vietnam talking about all the paranoia, saying they never knew who the enemy was . . . this whole deal about the little girls who could be Vietcong. Shit. It started before they even got over there. The first enemies were their good buddies who convinced them to enlist. The assholes on their draft boards. Their parents and brothers and teachers and the VFW. They all fucked them over . . . and when the guys got to Nam they hated them for it. They came home to the people who betrayed them, and they even loved them again, but the betrayal made them different. Once you've been fucked over by the infrastructure, you're never quite the same citizen. It was true for the ones that went and the ones that stayed."

He waited for them to say something and they didn't. Soon the silence was humiliating, because it said they didn't get what he'd said or didn't care enough to know more. Didn't have the connection. So he filled up the silence himself: "Anyway, it was a hell of a lot easier being here than there. No one gets his ass blown off on a psych ward. I didn't have to kill anyone." He pulled up to Wilkerson's house. "Here we are. Get ready."

Cars and trucks were parked on both sides of the street and the latest arrivals were skittering up the driveway through the rain.

It's true, he thought. The whole congregation gets to hear everything that Leo had to say. If Leo was crazy or desperate at the end, anything could be written out in a few minutes. Chuck felt no anxiety, though. Leo's discretion and stoicism were stronger than his heart and bone. His body would have failed him first.

And anyway, there was nowhere to run.

"How come you never told us anything about this? About being in the hospital?" his wife asked. He looked at her now. She wasn't angry or hurt, but she was squinting in disbelief. Even squinting, her brown eyes looked huge.

"It was a long time ago. It was a different universe. Why would you care?"

"But I asked you once, at Lane and Marion's. You said you had a high lottery number."

"It was a lie of convenience. The truth takes about ten minutes to tell," he said. "Most people can't sit still that long."

# Six

The grayness had thickened during the half-mile drive from the village center to the lawyer's house—still mostly clouds, now mixed with a wintry dusk. By the time they had pulled up in front of the half-bricked rambler, Gretchen could barely read the sign, driven into the front lawn: Wilkerson Law Offices.

She got out of the car and had taken steps up the sidewalk before she realized that she was alone. Everyone else was walking up the wide cement driveway, toward the white light emanating from the double garage. In a row: Chuck, Kara, a shrunken, limping white-haired wraith. The old woman was supported by a big-boned woman: fortyish, bad perm, wearing a dirty pink parka. Gretchen scurried across the wet lawn, catching up with them as they reached the brownish-gray folding chairs, which,

45

she thought, would be called taupe if they were anything other than folding chairs.

Most of the chairs were already occupied. Chuck worked his way through the crowd to a group of empty seats at the side nearest the house, next to a heavy workbench. The bench was clean and all the tools were hung on Peg-Board. Gretchen noted that the handsaw was supported with two pegs through the handle, one lower than the other, so that the saw hung straight down. A fluorescent light glared from over the bench, and another lit the front of the garage, above a small lectern.

A man leaned over beside the lectern, his hand resting on it, talking with a woman in the front row. Everything Gretchen could see of him was rounded—the ball of his blond head, the arch of his back, the puffy balloon hand on the lectern. He didn't straighten up but seemed to roll the huge orb of his body back on top of his legs. His face was as smooth as an apple. For all his bulk, though, he was meticulously dressed. The flesh on his neck didn't spill over his collar but was cradled gently by it; his charcoal suit jacket rested across his bowed shoulders without stretching; his pants weren't splayed flat against his abdomen but projected slightly, the pleats crisp.

Gretchen approved of the effort. It took discipline and self-esteem for an obese man to look so nice. She wondered how such a person had become obese in the first place.

"It's such a tidy garage," she whispered to her daughter. It reminded her of a good classroom—full of tools, echoing of recent activity, but ordered. Still, she thought, it was no one's fantasy to have his last testament read in the shadow of his lawyer's old lawn furniture.

Wilkerson scanned the room and his eyes registered on Chuck. He cleared his throat.

"It's four-thirty," he said. "I notice that Chuck is here, so we should get started. Would someone step around back and tell all the guys who are littering my yard with cigarette butts to get in here?"

Shuffling feet and the scraping of chairs over cement. She looked back. Gromek the ferry captain leaned against a wall at the back of the garage. A man with a reddish-brown beard and aviator glasses stood beside him. Out on the driveway, the red-lipped blonde from the bar (another bad perm, Gretchen thought) planted her feet and slipped her hands into the pockets of a blue satin baseball jacket. A tall man with watery eyes hovered near her.

"Come on inside, Jeanine," Wilkerson said. "There are a few seats here in front."

Chuck turned to look but nothing showed on his face. Jeanine smiled thinly at the lawyer but didn't move.

Wilkerson cleared his throat again. "First, I'll apologize for the humble venue and—especially—the absence of heat. Suffice it to say that I usually play to a smaller crowd when I host a will reading. I will endeavor to be speedy." He tapped a red folder. "I have here the last will and testament of Leo Hausman. I have the legal document, and I have a letter, which is somewhat less formal in language and gets to the heart of what Leo wanted to say to you all. I'll read the letter first." He pulled several sheets of ruled paper out of the folder and began to read.

August 14

Dear friends and family,

    The money is gone. Gone. Gone.

    I have more to say but I know that some of you want

to know about the money first. I have no desire to make you wait in suspense while I discourse on faith and love. So there you have it. The money is gone. It was invested according to plan, poorly but with good intent. We tried to shield our small wealth from the predations of the great banking cabal and fell prey to a smaller but equally vicious conspiracy. We lost everything except the receipt of deposit from a Bahamian bank which no longer exists.

I am embarrassed by this. Humiliated. And deeply saddened, because I know how that money might have improved your lives and the lives of your families. Anything I could do to get that money back to you, I'd do it. But I am tired and sick and not much thinking about the physical world.

Speaking of the physical world, I'll announce my bequests here. (This is detailed in the will, but you'll all be gossiping about it anyway, so we might as well get the cards on the table.)

To Corrine Ford, I give the little money I have in the bank.

Wilkerson paused. "This next sentence is in capital letters, and then it goes on regular."

THIS IS MY MONEY FROM MANY YEARS AGO AND WAS NOT CONNECTED TO CASTLE RAMPARTS BANK. Corrine can also have the house to live in as long as she's alive and able to live there, unless she prefers to live in her own place. Whenever she doesn't want to live in the house, or can't live in it, or dies, it goes to Chuck. He can sell it or live in it—whatever he chooses.

Chuck also gets the furnishings, all my Ojibwa arti-facts, the crystal, and anything else of value in the house and on the property. It's not much of a legacy but whatever he can find is his.

To Pete Gromek, I leave my books.

To Art Sannar, I leave my records. My musical records, that is. My personal records go to Chuck. Church records go to the sorry bastard who follows me there.

This is the part where I discourse on faith and love, but I find I don't have the energy for it this evening.


"There's a break in the letter here," Wilkerson said. "Then it picks up again the following day."


August 15

This is a big day in the Catholic Church, the Feast of the Annunciation. An angel—make that an archangel, as if being an angel isn't holy enough, as if there's a point to a hierarchy of angels—anyway the archangel tells the Virgin Mary she's with child.

I used to mock the Catholic faith. Now I think it's not so bad. It's bizarre but you can get your arms around it. The squirrelly old aunt of religions.

I don't know if sickness is making me spiritually feeble, or if the inevitability of death—and the weird-ness of it—lets me appreciate the strangeness of Catholics. Next I'll be reading up on Buddhism.

Odd how the mind shifts around when you are dy-ing. Odd and frightening. When you are well, you think you know how you will face death. You make those assumptions and prepare for this based on those assumptions. Then you get sick and suddenly you aren't that person anymore. The assumptions don't apply. The approach of death changes you and it is this entirely new person who is facing death. The old you is already dead.

This is a source of hope for some, I suppose.

That old me is already dead. All of you can hate him—in a way, I hate him too. But don't hate the man I am now. It was that other man who hurt you. Especially you, Chuck. It was that other man who ruined your life with Mary, who ruined your chance at happiness.

I would do anything to make that up to you. I would commit any lesser sin . . . I would lie, or steal . . . if I thought it would help. But I know that anything I can do will be too little. I am sorry.

The man who might have hurt you—all of you—is dead, and if there is a hell, that man is surely in it.

This dying is hard. I am too tired and sad and strange to myself.

Wilkerson paused for a moment. Cleared his throat again. "There's a break and then another paragraph," he said softly. Kara looked up at her mother, questioning. Gretchen did not reply but nodded toward the lawyer, who began speaking again.

October 12

It has taken me a long time to get back to this. I just read the last part that I wrote and realize I was mistaken. It wasn't the Annunciation. It was the Assumption, the day the Virgin Mary got sucked up to heaven.

I've taken so much from you all. I wish I had more to give. I beg you all to search . . . please search my legacy and I hope you will find some of what you've given me returned to you. I have received so much from you . . . and now I want to give it back. Chuck, my son and heir, must help. There is so much you can do to repay them, Chuck.

Once again, I'm too exhausted to get to the faith and love.

"Well." Wilkerson slid the letter back into the red folder. "That was as far as Leo got. As I mentioned, I have the actual legal document and I'll need to go over it with . . ."

"What a load of crap," Gromek said, his squealing voice rising above the lawyer's.

Wilkerson arched a thin eyebrow. "I beg your pardon?"

"Well, did the crazy old bastard have our money or not?"

Wilkerson pulled out the letter again without taking his eyes off Gromek. He read: " 'The money is gone. Gone. Gone.' What part of that don't you understand?"

"Sure, he says that." Gromek talked as he pushed his way into the garage. "Then he says he wishes there was some way to get the money back to us but he can't think of it and then he gives his kid a house with two hundred yards of lakefront that's worth a good part of what he took offa us in his crazy bank scheme."

"I suppose you could sue the estate," Wilkerson began, but Gromek cut him off.

"Yeah and pay more money to more goddamn lawyers. What I want to know is, does he have our money hidden somewhere or not? He gives the kid the house and calls it his legacy . . . and then he tells us to go search his legacy for some way to repay what he owes us. And he says he can't really repay the kid for wrecking his life, but he would steal if it would help." Gromek pulled his cap off and wiped his thinning hair with his hand. "What an absolutely fucking old crazy old bastard."

"Yeah, and what about giving Waterboy all the valuables on the property?" This was a nasal voice, which Gretchen saw belonged to the red-bearded man. "What the hell does that mean? That the money is around somewhere or what?"

Despite the cool of the open garage, Wilkerson took off his suit coat and hung it squarely on the back of a folding chair. "Look," he said, rolling up the sleeves. "I'm going to be very honest about this. Chuck, I hope you'll forgive me if something sounds indelicate. Leo Hausman was old and sick and under a lot of pressure when he wrote this." Wilkerson stopped and laughed at himself. "Under a lot of pressure? Shit, he was about forty-eight hours from being dead. He said himself that he was half crazed.

"Now, if you're thinking about digging up the woods around his house—the house that is now, essentially, Chuck's house—I don't recommend it. First, from a legal standpoint, it's trespassing. Second, from a practical standpoint, it'll be a lot of hard work ... and you aren't going to find diddly. Leo said it as clearly as it can be said in the most lucid part of this letter. The money is gone, gone, gone. He felt bad. Now *he's* gone, gone, gone. Case closed."

"Bullshit." Gromek scowled at him. "There's more here. I can smell it."

The bearded man with the nasal voice said, "I can smell it too."

Wilkerson extended an arm to the other corner of the garage. "Lyle, do you have anything to add here?"

Gretchen turned, following the line of sight of the woman behind her.

The man leaning against the garage doorframe said nothing for several long seconds, then slowly drew himself up. His hard leather soles rasped on the cement. Keys jangled. He took so long to speak that her attention shifted and she placed a hand on Chuck's leg, tapped him once, needing to ask now, in the first open moment: Who the hell was Mary? Chuck didn't respond. He kept his eyes on Lyle, who had straightened up and was now so tall that his thick dark hair threatened to scrape the edge of the suspended garage door. "No," he said. He gave a quarter turn to the wide-brimmed sheriff's hat in his hands.

"OK, then," Wilkerson said.

"Except," Lyle went on, "that no one should get any ideas about going out to the Hausman place. Any of you"—here he gestured with the hat toward Gromek—"have a problem with that?"

In the silent moment that followed, Gretchen turned back to the lawyer and found herself facing the white-haired wraith. The hair, she saw now, was a wig.

"Leo wouldn't have liked this," the old woman whispered. "He was a gentle man." Gretchen nodded. The woman stuck her neck out and a thin cloud of stale perfume—the smell of old Kleenex—floated off her. The old woman made her voice even softer. "He was so pale at the end, you could almost see through him," she confided, nodding.

Gretchen nodded back.

"I have nothing more to add," Wilkerson said. "I'll go

over the formal will now, and you're all welcome to stay." Chuck stood and pushed aside chairs as he approached the lawyer. Gretchen started to follow but suddenly Chuck was back, saying, "I have to tell you something." He took her elbow and directed her first to the side of the garage. He stopped, changed his mind, directed her outside, next to a large pine tree in the front yard. Night had fallen while they were in the garage, but she could see him clearly in the light from the ornate fixture over Wilkerson's front door.

"Look . . . ," he began. Then: "Kara! Come here. Come over here." When she was a few feet away, he said, "I have to tell your mom something and you should hear it too. I should have told you about the draft. You want to know everything and now that we're a family you've got a right to know it. So you should also know that I was married before." Gretchen felt herself floating. "That girl named Mary, the one Leo mentioned in the letter. We were married about six months and then she died. Drowned. Her car went through the ice driving over to the mainland."

He turned away from them for a moment and she thought he was going to walk back to the car. She wondered if she could move. Then he turned back. "I feel lousy about this, OK? This was a lousy way for you to hear about it. It's my fault. But it's not easy for me to talk about."

She thought it odd that she had nothing to say. She didn't feel an urge to yell at him. Or hit him. Or sympathize with him. She just stared at his face and hair and would have continued to do so if Lyle hadn't approached and spoken.

"Excuse me," he said softly. He hesitated, waiting to see if they had more to say to each other, and in the pause she noticed that he must have cut himself shaving earlier in the day. He had a big, angular jaw and she stared at it, thinking: How odd to have just heard about your husband's previous marriage and yet what really seems to have captivated you is this razor cut on a stranger. She could see the nick under his ear and a thread of dried brown blood on the collar of his gray shirt.

"I just wanted you to know that I was sad about your father's passing," he said finally. "If there's anything I can do ..." He waved his big brown hat toward the garage. "Those guys talk a lot, do a little. I wouldn't worry about them, but if you need me ..."

He set the hat gently on his head, then gave it a tug forward. "I'd sure be surprised if Leo had even a few dollars of that money left. It just wasn't in his nature." He paused. "Not like him. At all."

"Are you playing detective with me, Lyle?"

Lyle said nothing, just stared straight forward, into the darkness over their heads. "Anyway, my condolences."

Gretchen noticed the ruby-lipped bartender, hands still buried in her jacket, standing at the edge of the driveway. As Lyle passed her, he nodded and said, "Jeanine." She nodded back, then stared at Gretchen and Kara and Chuck. She lowered her eyes, but didn't move. She stood there. Maybe waiting, Gretchen thought. Maybe paralyzed. Maybe just available.

Chuck ignored her. "We gotta get out of here," he said. "If anyone tries to talk to you, pretend like you don't hear them or see them." They walked quickly to the Subaru, climbed in. Chuck put the key in the ignition, started the motor, then pounded the steering wheel once. "Shit, I've got to tell Wilkerson something." He killed the engine. "Wait here." He opened the door, jumped out, pushed down the door lock on his side. "Lock it up," he said.

She punched down the door lock, heard Kara do the same. Watched him slip away into the darkness.

"Hey, Mom."

She turned to her daughter, waited. When Kara didn't speak, she said, "What am I supposed to do, honey?"

"I'm sixteen. What do I know about this stuff?"

Kara was huddled into the corner of the back seat. She was cold. Gretchen wondered why Chuck had turned the car off, walked away with the keys. "I'm going to start the engine," she said. "It'll warm us up." She fished her keys out of her purse.

"How you doing, Mom?"

"I'm not sure." She started the car—awkwardly— from the passenger seat. "I'm . . . I don't know."

"You want to talk about it? You should make the effort, you know. You've said that. You've said that it's important to try to communicate, even when you're not sure what's going to come out."

"Jesus, you're going to give that to me now?" Her voice rose; she couldn't stop it. "Where was all this deep feeling about sharing last summer, when I didn't know where you were every other night and whenever I asked I got whatever line of bullshit was the easiest to palm off on me? I'm not an idiot, you know."

Kara said nothing.

People continued to filter out of the garage. A few were knotted on the front lawn, orange cigarette tips glowing in the dark. One of the smokers flicked his cigarette periodically, letting loose what appeared to be a single spark each time.

"You wouldn't tell me where you were," Gretchen said.

"That was different."

A shadow jogged across the street to them, rapped on

the window. She opened the door and Chuck slipped behind the wheel, groaning.

"What is it?" she asked, her voice now drained of emotion.

"How come I get to be part of so many people's histories when they're not part of mine." He punched the clutch, jammed the shift lever forward, but didn't release the clutch. "People go up to rock-and-roll stars every day and say: Hey, I listened to your music constantly when I was getting married or divorced or when I was in jail or the war or whatever. OK, being part of people's lives is part of their job. They picked it. It's not part of my job. I don't want people making me part of their history when I'm not trying to be."

A few hours earlier, cartoonish ranting like this would have seemed unconsciously charming. Male anger that was vehement but not threatening. Over lunch, it might have elicited her sympathy. Under her present circumstances, though, his charm was a useless attribute. She felt only fatigue. And a queasy sense of danger.

Still, she asked, "What are you talking about?"

"Nothing." He turned on the lights. Just as he was about to pull away from the curb, an orange pickup rumbled alongside them and stopped, blocking their exit, and the window glass rolled slowly down on the passenger's side.

Oh Jesus, she thought. This is it. Next the shotgun barrel comes sliding through the window. She inhaled deeply—more a gasp than a breath—and put her hand on her husband's shoulder.

"Art," he said. He rolled down his window. "What's up?"

"I was wondering if you guys are going to go back to Leo's? I thought maybe I'd get Brian and we'd stop by. Pick up my records. Make sure everything is copacetic."

"Great. Thanks. Come now and have supper with us."

"You got it." He wound up the window and pulled ahead of them.

"Jesus," Gretchen said. "I thought that was it."

"What?"

"I thought someone was going to kill you."

"Honey, honey." He patted her hand. "This isn't the urban jungle." He eased off the clutch and as the car rolled ahead he winked at her, the dashboard lights casting an orange reflection on the open eye. "Up here, you don't kill people out where everyone can see it." He shifted gears. "We consider it a private matter."

# Wilkerson

*The law is no job for the squeamish.*

*To do it well, you must dissect people—clients and opponents alike. You nose around them. You turn over their clammy bedding. You prod the garbage in their rank cellars. You get on your hands and knees. You put an eye on the plane of the tiles on their kitchen floor to see what agglomerations of dust and hair are casting shadows there. You spread yourself invitingly to accept unbidden revelations.*

*I am hired help, but people readily throw down the curtains and expose their private lives, even though that glimpsing embarrasses us both. No voyeuristic juice is squeezed from these displays. For the most part, they are shocking only in the depth of their pettiness. The lack of self-respect they indicate. I dislike them as much as I dislike waking people at odd hours and seeing their ratty pajamas.*

*For the same reason, I abhor public events like Leo's*

*will reading. It brings out the pettiness. The bickering and clawing at each other.*

*They can't get along, but not one of them could stand on his own feet. All the denim and 4 × 4s, all the raw-boned rhetoric and survivalist arcana, and yet their destinies are linked as closely as bees, as ants, as coral. They are a colony in this sense: they are beings in droves.*

*And they hate it. The lethal insult here is to tell a man he is dependent. And when someone acknowledges that she needs another being, that she craves union—she is exploited and abandoned. By the big men like Bartok and the little men like Blaylock. By the Reverend Leo Haus-man, who was so overtaken by grief at the passing of his young wife that he spent the next thirty years trying to spike every hole, plug every aperture, jam every cavity.*

*They use and discard, all of them. Not me: I am a con-servationist when it comes to romance and flesh-pleasure. I never throw anything away. I have my photos, my me-mentos, my little friend. (She bores me now—old things never shine—but I foresee no changes. Reduce, reuse, re-cycle. It becomes easier with age.)*

*But if I find this colonial life repellent, why did I be-come an attorney, parsing the rules of the hive? Because it promised a modicum of security in a world that should be indifferent to one's fate, but seems inexplicably tilted toward malevolence.*

*Because I truly cannot see another way for me. And I have looked: I have seen how simply a man can live in Vanuatu and Nauru. In the Caribbean, it's the same. Even the money people I've worked with in the Caymans and the Bahamas can somehow live with less.*

*Oh, Jah. I'm sorry, but I and I don't buy it.*

*Among the people on this island, I also see a kind of*

*antimaterialism. They latch eyes on a new snowmobile-fishing boat-shotgun; they want these things; they lie and steal and whine until they get them; and then they lose interest. Everything in the physical world becomes an extension of themselves, and because they hate themselves, they hate what they own.*

*Listen to me. Sigmund Freud.*

*If they are so cavalier about material objects, why the stink about the money that dried up in Nassau? Because they have felt what it is like to exploit—virtually rape—and abandon someone, and now they cannot bear the idea that they have been used so loosely?*

*And here's the humiliating part: They all think it was Leo who did the buggering. To see Bartok at Leo's side those last weeks, the dutiful amateur male nurse, hanging on any word or sign from that sick old man that might tell him where the money was. Then to realize that the life had seeped out of Leo before the truth. And then to be so cruelly re-jilted at the will reading. Buggered and buggered again. Little wonder that Bartok is in a dark mood.*

*Still, it's entertaining to see one of them actually betray an emotion, even one as murderous as Bartok's. They think of themselves as a taciturn and stoic lot, but they are just poor communicators. A real stoic holds back; these people don't know how to clear their throats.*

*I think that's why young Hausman deranged them so. Here was a young man who was apparently not holding back. He was being as loudly mad as he could be without overselling it. He spilled his guts—or what he claimed were his guts—at every opportunity. Not a subtle performance, but subtlety was not a characteristic of the times. A muted performance brought basic training, not accolades.*

*(Am I confident that he was faking it? Absolutely.)*

The irony, of course, is that he was—is—the most enigmatic of them all. Instead of the local pretense of stoicism, he donned the most bizarre and distracting camouflage. Like those ships in World War II that were painted in bright cubist designs; because the U-boat captain couldn't interpret the splash of color on the horizon, he dismissed it without consciously registering it—or so the theory went. Chuck Hausman hid by drawing attention to himself. Decidedly not like his young stepdaughter, who tries to deflect attention from her body with baggy men's pants and that oversized, tit-hiding sweater.

Hausman's genius was that he had the emotional discipline to stay in character. Even today. You couldn't tell what he was feeling.

When the others drop their pretense of stoicism and actually do let go, you see how little they've mastered the art of emotional restraint. You see this utter lack of self-control that they try to palm off as passion. Perhaps I'm being unfair. Maybe it is passion.

I'm the attorney; I don't mean to judge. Bless their twisted emotions and the clutter and bloodshed that spews from them. Here, after all, is where I make a living.

# Seven

OK, Chuck thought, I could have handled that better.

He had no desire to lie to her. But he didn't want to tell anyone something they didn't want to hear. For some people, truth was like a National Park: expansive, open for everyone to explore, publicly maintained. For him, truth was dark and intimate and as labyrinthine as sex. Like sex, he didn't share it with just anyone. And he didn't share it with people who weren't able to appreciate it.

Of course, he couldn't tell her that.

He drove slowly over the rain-washed roads because this would take some time and he wanted it finished before they got to the house. It was a family affair and nothing for Mrs. Ford's ears and eyes. Or Art's. "I'm sorry. I screwed up. I did this all wrong. I'm sorry."

"OK," she said.

"The draft thing was bad, but it's not that big a deal.

People did so much weird shit back then, and it was all done without the least embarrassment. And now a lot of it is stuff you just don't want to talk about."

"I don't want to talk about this now."

"OK, but I want to say that I think it was a big deal that I didn't say anything about Mary. If I'd stopped to think about it, I'd have known that we couldn't come up here and go through the will reading and not have you find out. But it was just something I'd pushed out of my head. It was this short, weird period in my life. Two wild kids. I never even think about it. It's like I have repressed memory syndrome."

"OK."

"No, it's not OK. But the point is that I was institutionalized because I wasn't so crazy I wanted to go to Vietnam, but I am not mentally well when it comes to Mary's death."

She folded her hands. Her fingers were as long and elegant as her legs, and he enjoyed watching them fidget in her lap. "And what the hell do I say to that?"

"I wish you'd say you forgive me, even if you don't understand it all. And, Kara, I wish you'd do the same. You had a right to know too. And on top of that, I've dragged you into a lot of adult neurotic behavior that you shouldn't have to be exposed to yet."

Neither of them answered. That told him Gretchen was weakening. He could smell it.

He glanced back at Kara, who shrugged. "Look," she said. "You're not the first grown-up who's lied to me. Or held back telling the truth. I'm not that shocked by it. Or by the fact that you had a wife before. I know a lot of people who have had previous relationships, OK?"

"Well, I'm still sorry. I don't want to be that kind of grown-up. I don't want us to have that kind of family."

He waited a beat, then let it fly. But softly: "And I have one other announcement."

"Oh, Jesus," Gretchen wailed. "What's left? You've got a family in . . . *Samoa*? I can't take this."

"This has nothing to do with me. It has to do with all of us. Or it could. I just want to get it on the table." He inhaled deeply. "All that money that Leo lost? I don't think he lost it. I think it's in the house. Or nearby."

Gretchen lifted her eyes to the sun visor.

"No way," said Kara. She was smiling. "He was a minister. They were his congregation."

Chuck shook his head. "First, Leo was a bastard. Second, his only real interest was power. Religion and politics were just a means to that end. Money would have had the same appeal but he never had the chance to be corrupted by it—at least not when I knew him. Third, this offshore banking deal was such an easy scam. All these gun-toting-survivalist-fringe-right-Posse-Comitatus-bullshit-bullshit-assholes think the world is run by a bunch of Jewish bankers. And they won't pay taxes. They try to run a cash economy. All their money goes in their mattresses or they run it through weird tax scams and offshore accounts. They'd jump at a Bahamian bank account or whatever Leo was hawking."

Gretchen stared at him. "You knew nothing about this before today?"

"You suppose Leo would write me a letter about it? Dear Chuck, ripped off my buddies today. But you know, I bet he did write it up in his diary. The son of a bitch kept an unbelievable journal. Spent hours at it every night, keeping track of the day's events, every dime he made, every dime he spent. At the end of the year—and this was without a spreadsheet program, by the way—he'd be able to tell you . . . Jesus."

"What? What is it?"

"That was it. He said . . . oh, he was such a sneaky bastard . . . he started by saying that Art could have his records and then . . . like it's an afterthought, he says, of course, Chuck gets my personal records . . . the diary, in other words. That's where he tells us where he hid the money."

"But he hated you," Kara said. "He hated the idea of you. Those are your words, by the way. So why would he want to give you the money?"

"Blood . . . is deeper than justice," he sang.

"Is that Springsteen?" Gretchen asked.

"No. Maybe it was blood. Maybe it was justice. Leo made my life hell, and he made my marriage to Mary impossible." He felt his voice waver, so slightly that he thought they might have missed it. He stopped talking, just long enough to purge the emotion, then said, "He ruined any chance of happiness we could have had. He knew it. And after Mary drowned, I think he held himself liable. I think it was the only guilt he ever felt in this life. It wouldn't surprise me that he might try to make up for it with money."

"Money that he stole?" Gretchen asked. "From the people who most trusted him?"

"Who else was he gonna rob? The people who didn't trust him?"

"Well, that's just perfect," Gretchen sighed. "On top of everything else, now Lyle gets to tell us to hang around a week while he sorts things out. Meanwhile, a mob of peasants descends on the house with picks and shovels and flaming torches. You can just see this fresh hell coming at us, can't you?"

"Well, we have to make a choice here, don't we?"

"Excuse me?"

"We have to choose between fresh hell and sin."

He pulled the car into the gravel patch in front of the house, the headlights glaring back at him in the front window. He killed the lights, turned to face her and Kara. He spoke slowly. "Kara, I want to start by saying this is an ambivalent moral situation. In a pure world, we would find the money, give it back to the fine people who rightly own it, and it would be a great story to tell the folks back home. And we might want to do that.

"On the other hand, suppose you're a poor Cambodian farmer. You find all the golden eyeglass frames the Khmer Rouge pulled from the faces of the people they killed? Do you give them back to Pol Pot? Do you give back wealth to your persecutors?

"These people persecuted me. They mocked me, beat me, treated me like a freak since I was in nursery school. They tried as hard as they could to send me to Vietnam and they would have been delighted if I'd wound up scattered under half a dozen palm trees. When they couldn't do that, they sent me to an unspeakable snake-pit psycho ward.

"So, yeah, we might want to give the money back. But don't talk to me about whether it's right or wrong to keep it. If I gave it back, I'd feel just as dirty as if I kept it."

It was already more than he wanted to say, but he couldn't stop himself.

"And as a practical matter, we're going to need that money if you ever want to get your little safe house in the suburbs, because Leo gave this house to Mrs. Ford until she's dead or infirm and Mrs. Ford is pig-strong. By the time we get a chance to sell this place and stop being urban pioneers, Kara will be out of the house and living on a sailboat in Sausalito."

He couldn't see Gretchen's eyes in the dark, but her voice was steely: "Why are you talking to me like this? Are you trying to scare me? Are you trying to intimidate me?"

"You don't like it when I don't tell you the scary stuff. I thought I'd try it the other way." He scratched his nose. He'd run out of things to say. "Let's have supper and get our bearings here. Maybe we won't be able to find the diary anyway."

# Eight

Her mother had told her to inventory the basement. To search for antiques and other modest treasures that might have been tucked in the corners or hidden under the workbench. Kara also thought her mother wanted her out of the way while she and the others made supper and talked. Under other circumstances she might have taken offense at this, but tonight she went willingly into the cold and dark. She wanted to be out of the way. Craved a fresh rinse of unconnectedness.

The basement was a walkout. One wall was buried in the hill above the beach; the wall opposite was set with windows that looked out on the lake. A door opened out to a path that led down to the water. She tried the handle, found it unlocked, but wasn't able to budge the door. Then she noticed the dead bolt, high up the side of the door, and slid it back. Immediately, the door seemed to sag, and the next gust of wind knocked it against the wooden frame with a deep thonk.

Outside, the cold quickly penetrated her sweater and jeans. She fingered a cigarette from her T-shirt, lit it, inhaled deliciously. Someone had told her it wasn't enjoyable to smoke in the dark. What bullshit. It was wonderful. And if time still passed with aching arthritic slowness, at least it had shape and color in it. You took a drag and let it out and there—that was a small brushstroke of time. It wasn't much but it kept time from coming at you one excruciating pixel after another.

After four or five drags, the enjoyment succumbed to the cold. She tossed the butt and went back inside, locking the door behind her so that it quit rattling. On a nice day, she thought, the windows would have given the room plenty of air, if they'd ever been opened. And light, if the curtains had been pulled aside. This hadn't happened recently, however. The smell of mildew was already seeping into her clothes, and the basement's surfaces were thick with undisturbed dust.

In the dim light, she searched the corners and found nothing of interest or value: a stack of empty cardboard boxes that cluttered the base of the stairs; a workbench littered with tools and half-empty cans of paint and sealants; disorganized drawers of fishing tackle; rusty metal cabinets full of rusty wrenches; an oak chair with one shattered leg; a small laundry area where Mrs. Ford had pushed back the crud and chaos, where a pair of orange-and-green-flowered sheets now hung, moist and still.

The last place she inspected was the tiny chamber under the stairs. She picked up a flashlight from the workbench, put her free hand on the metal hasp. Felt the raised flakes of rust rough on her fingertips. Shivered. Pulled. The door creaked.

The first impression was of dreadful metal teeth, then cobwebs. More teeth and dirt and cobwebs. Traps, some of them big enough for the biggest animals she could imagine. She could see no rust on them but they were thick with webs—heavy, collapsed webs, long abandoned. She let her light's beacon drift down. A neat pile of split firewood and, next to it, a jumble of thin branches and kindling.

She heard the door open at the head of the stairs.

"Mom? Is that you?" she called.

She heard no answer, but just above her head, footsteps were making their way quickly down the stairs. She turned sharply, caught a spiderweb across her chest, and stepped into the light. Without thinking, she'd raised the flashlight in one hand while she pawed the sticky threads off her face. The light bounced wildly around the room and her mother called out. "Kara?"

Gretchen turned at the base of the stairs, then tripped over a tattered lawn chair. She caught herself on a shelf of jars—each filled with a sampling of nuts, bolts, and nameless doodads—shaking it violently and nearly knocking the contents to the floor.

"Jeez! This is dangerous."

"You OK?" Kara asked.

"Yes, I thought you were . . ." She brushed her hands. "Find anything?"

"Just junk. Not even garage-sale quality."

Gretchen sighed, glancing quickly around the big room. "No surprise, I guess. Nasty down here, isn't it?" Kara shrugged. "Come on. Supper's almost ready."

Kara followed her upstairs, into the kitchen. She heard

Art and Chuck talking in the living room; Brian sat quietly nearby.

Her mother cut vegetables for a salad. Kara washed her hands at the kitchen sink, glancing out at the lake. The kitchen light cast a faint glow on the beach, allowing her to see—faintly—a figure moving across the sand toward the wooden stairs. It was wearing a long coat and, Kara now saw, a dress. There was no mistaking the heavy stride, the long gray pennants of hair lofted by the wind. The old woman was pulling herself up the stairway now, one stair at a time.

"Mom," Kara said, pointing toward the back door. "She's back. Mrs. Ford."

Her mother mimed a scream and quickly pushed the cut carrots into the salad bowl. "Make her go away," she said.

"Mom."

It was a scold and Gretchen, accepting it, raised her hands. "OK, OK. My job." She went to the back door and opened it just as the old woman reached the landing. Kara could see that while she had changed her dress, she had not bothered to iron it. Her face was drawn. She walked into the room, still wearing her coat, and Kara caught a whiff of something sour.

"How are you, Mrs. Ford?" her mother asked. Kara leaned against the cabinets, eager to see how her mother would handle the old housekeeper.

"I'm not so good," she replied. It was not a protest; just a statement of fact, followed by another: "I'm here to make dinner."

"Oh *thanks*, Mrs. Ford," her mother said too sweetly, "but we've already taken care of everything." This is going to be a show, thought Kara. Perky Mom fending off the Kitchen Hag.

Gretchen continued: "You're welcome to stay, of course."

"You've what?"

"Well, we got hungry so we just started cooking."

"Of course." Mrs. Ford stood next to the kitchen table and folded her arms; she stared blankly at the floor. "A person works in a house for thirty years, cooking every night, and it . . ." She stopped.

"I can imagine."

"No. I don't think you can, young lady."

Mrs. Ford took off her coat, folded it over her arm. "Oh, what am I talking about? It's your kitchen now. You do as you please." She turned toward Kara, then back to Gretchen. "But I wouldn't get too comfortable here."

The old woman trembled then, and Kara saw something pass into her. She could not describe it but she could see it enter one side of the old woman's body and fill her. Then it was gone. "Nothing that ever happened in this house was comfortable," Mrs. Ford said. She laughed and sat down hard.

Chuck appeared in the doorway, an empty beer bottle in hand. "Hi, Mrs. Ford." He set the empty on the counter. "You should have gone to the will reading, you know. It concerned you." She tsked, looked away. He smiled at her and put his hands in his back pockets. "I don't know how much Leo discussed this with you. You knew that he gave you rights to the house for as long as you want to live here?"

"No. He never talked to me about it. And after?"

"It goes back to the family. To me. You also get all his money in the bank, whatever that adds up to." He wiped his mouth with his hand. "To know how much that is, I'll need to go over his financial records. I couldn't find them upstairs, by the way. Did you ever happen to see them?"

"Financial records, no." Her head wagged. She was far away.

"How about his diary? He used to keep track of all his finances in his diary."

She snapped back to the present. "His diary? You can't have his diary."

"Why not?"

"It's his diary." She stood up slowly now, supporting herself on the edge of the table. "No one can look in his diary."

Chuck frowned. "I guess I have to make that decision, Mrs. Ford. You got the money . . . the money in the bank. Whatever bank that might be. But Leo left me all his records, and I'd say that includes his diary."

"I disagree."

Chuck's frown eased into a smile of disbelief. "It's not for you to agree or disagree. The diary's mine. If you do anything to keep me from getting it, Mrs. Ford, you'll be breaking the law . . . and going against Leo's last wishes."

The old woman turned to Gretchen, who was sliding cut tomatoes onto the spinach and carrots already in the salad bowl. "Here, dear," she said. "Let me help you with that."

When Kara went out to set the table, Brian stood up and shuffled over. His bright blue eyes were so wet she wanted to dab them with one of the napkins in her hand.

"Can Brian help?" he said cheerily.

She grinned at him. "Brian can get the glasses."

He put his hands firmly on a chair back. "Brian prefers not to."

"Oh? And why not?"

"People are arguing in there."

She leaned close to him to lay out the silverware and caught the bitter aroma of wood smoke. "It's just a conversation, I think."

Brian shook his head so that a heavy lock of graying hair slid over his ears. He brushed it back. "They're arguing over Leo's diary. I was listening. It's funny."

"Funny?"

"Funny peculiar. Leo was a big shot. A hero hereabouts. But what does the hero leave behind? Arguments. You know what they say? 'Unhappy the land that needs heroes.'"

She placed the last setting and looked up at him. "You're an interesting person."

Brian beamed. "People used to say that more when I was younger. But when you're older and you're interesting, they think you're an idiot. They think I'm, like, 'Tell me about the rabbit, George.'"

"Excuse me?"

Brian grimaced. "It's from *Of Mice and Men*."

"I don't think so."

"The cartoon one." He sighed. "Anyway, they don't get me. I'm more complicated than they know." He winked solemnly. "I have insights."

"Really?" She winked back, thinking: Is this flirting? If it is, am I encouraging it? If I am, I'm doing so unconsciously, because I am not attracted to this man who is twenty-five years older than me. If I am flirting, it is really funny. Not funny ha-ha or funny peculiar. It is funny-bad-acid-help-me-I'm-lost-in-the-carpet.

Brian nodded gravely. "I know the pathology of this long epidemic of broken hearts." His eyebrows jerked up twice. He lowered his voice to a whisper. "I know the nature of all these incurable diseases of love."

"That sounds like a heavy burden, Brian."

"It comes with the territory. But I also have special talents that can relieve the weight of it all."

"Oh? Like what?"

He extended his thumb and finger to make a gun and pointed it at her. "I can walk over a chair." He glanced over his shoulder to make sure the others weren't watching and pulled out one of the wooden table chairs. "Check this out." He moved back a couple of steps, then walked straight toward the chair: the left foot on the ground, the right foot on the seat, the left foot rising toward the chair back.

She'd seen this done before. At this point, the person performing the trick was supposed to set his left foot on the chair's back, balance the chair on its rear legs, and slowly tip it backward, taking the last step on the floor. Done well, the movement was smooth, with a second of pleasant suspense as the chair dropped gently to the floor.

Brian's right foot hit the seat, his left foot rose and crashed into the chair back and it toppled over, slamming into the ground. Brian barreled into the wingback chair, bounced off, and rolled into the bookcase. When she came around the table she saw that one of the chair legs had been shattered.

The others streamed out of the kitchen, alarmed and chattering. Art stopped, looked around the room, and groaned, "Brian, you fucking idiot."

\* \* \*

It was that question Kara could never imagine herself asking, but had heard her mother ask several times, this time casually, both elbows propped on the faded blue tablecloth, the spaghetti-knotted fork suspended before her mouth, the laughter from something he'd said still decaying around them when she blurted out, "So, Art, why is it you never got married?" As if there were an answer that wasn't somehow humiliating or—if you were gay—awkward, because you had to explain your sexual orientation. The converse—"So, Frank, why is it you *got* married?"—seemed so much more intriguing and so rarely asked.

Art smirked and shrugged, which is what everyone did. Then he said, "I'm a selfish pig."

Her mother smiled around the mouthful of spaghetti. "That doesn't explain anything. Look at Chuck."

"And I never found a woman who liked really hot food. Every time I found someone and we had other stuff in common, there was this constant kitchen crisis." He tilted his head and looked at Kara. "From what I remember of sixteen, looks play a big part in who you're attracted to. Later in life, you want someone who's intellectually and emotionally simpatico. At my age, you need culinary compatibility."

Kara smiled but could think of nothing to say. The whole thing sounded phony to her. She looked for Mrs. Ford's reaction, but the old woman—seated by herself at the far end of the table—seemed not to have heard him. Art smiled back, not pushing her for a response.

"Hey," Brian said. "Are we just gonna eat and talk all night?"

"No," Art said. "We need drink too. A bottle of red, maybe. Leo kept a few bottles in the basement. Right,

Mrs. Ford?" The old woman shrugged. "Should I see what's lying around?" He pushed back his chair.

Kara couldn't recall any wine but said nothing. Chuck said, "It's weird how you know your way around my old house better than I do."

Art stopped in the doorway. "I used to get over here, you know, like four or five times a year. Church business or poker or whatever. Very low-key affairs, not like the old days. You know you're getting old when you start hanging with your friends' parents."

Kara heard him clomp down the stairs and, a moment later, return, climbing two at a time. "Leo must have moved the wine up here somewhere or drunk it all," he yelled from the refrigerator. He came back into the room with three beers and glanced sideways at Mrs. Ford, who didn't lift her head from her food. "Nothing there now. Too bad. Hot wine's nice on a cold night."

Colder now, Kara thought. A fresh gust came up, rattled the windows, and she heard a heavy thonking sound in a distant part of the house.

Art raised his beer bottle and said, "With full understanding that he was an s.o.b. for many of his seventy-one years, I propose a toast to Leo Hausman."

Chuck studied him. "Why? He was a jerk."

"I don't know. Because we all knew him. He was a big deal in our lives. Because he had a real effect on our lives."

"A real effect on our lives?" Mrs. Ford mocked him. "You mean he was a big buttinski."

"OK, sure," Art said. "And he was a jerk. We all have faults, and Leo had his." He set down the beer bottle without drinking from it. Instead, he sat back, pulled a pipe from his pocket, and loaded it with tobacco without asking if it was all right with everyone else.

"Everybody screws up all the time," he went on. "Gromek takes a drink on the ferry every so often. Poor Jeanine has her hopeless affairs. Bone Torkson shoplifts deodorant from the convenience store." He lit the pipe, puffed hard on it. "In Leo's case, it's amazing that people had so little to say for so long. Preacher lives in a fishbowl."

"Now that we-we've eaten, are we just gonna talk all night?" Brian asked.

"Not about Leo, we're not," Chuck said.

"You're right." Art shrugged. "OK, no toast. Enough sadness. Hey, you know what else I've seen in this house? In Leo's office or whatever it was, at the top of the stairs?" Art went on without waiting for Chuck. "Your old Gibson."

"Yesss," hissed Brian.

To Kara, Art explained, "Somewhere in his early travels, Chuck picked up one of the very early electric guitars. Kind of an amplified acoustic. From what? The forties?"

"Something like that."

"So," she said, "let me get this straight. You had a Triumph motorcycle and this classic electric guitar?"

"Yes. I thought I'd explained that I was a very cool guy."

"Still are, I'm sure," Art protested. "You still play, don't you?"

"Yes, yes," said Brian.

Chuck shook his head. "Not very much."

The smirk crossed Art's face again. "Feel up to it?"

"No way."

"Brian's got his ax in my truck. Mine's there, too."

"You're kidding."

Brian laughed. "Remember old man Kopke, sixty years old and still carrying his drum kit in his trunk?"

"We're not that bad," Art said. "But every once in a while . . . I don't know. I keep it handy. What do you say?" He turned to Gretchen. "Would you mind?"

"I'm sure I'd be very entertained," she said, with not quite enough irony for Kara's taste.

Art jumped up from the table, this time skipping stairs to the second floor. He was back in an instant, carrying a darkly varnished, beautifully curved guitar. It looked very much like a normal acoustic guitar, but thinner, and studded with two black dials.

Chuck pushed his chair back from the table and grinned. He set the old Gibson across his lap and stroked the strings easily. "You get pretty good sound from this even when it's not amplified," he said. "It's in tune. Leo or someone must have been playing it."

"I used to pick it up, once in a while," Mrs. Ford said quietly. "Didn't think you'd care."

Gretchen lowered one eyebrow and smiled. Kara couldn't tell if she was skeptical or just surprised. Chuck was not so condescending. "Not at all," he said. "I didn't know you played."

The old woman shrugged and returned to her food.

Art turned to Brian, saying, "I'll be back in a second."

Kara set her elbows firmly on the table and placed her face dolefully in her soft hands. "This is going to be a lot of hippie folk music, isn't it." Chuck shrugged and she raised her voice a key: "The first sign of Dave von Ronk, I'm out of here."

"You wouldn't know Dave von Ronk if I played him."

"Joni Mitchell, then." God, she thought, this is as bad as last summer. She leaned toward her mother and in something louder than a whisper she said, "You know, I'm the world's worst audience. I can't sit still and watch other people perform."

Gretchen winked at her. "Why don't you look around for a tambourine?"

"Tell me you never did that."

"I like music. I like taking part."

"There are things about a parent that a child should never know."

Kara's back was toward the door, so she didn't see Art coming in behind her. He handed Brian his instrument, saying, "Don't sit in Leo's chair."

"I know. I know."

Art came around the table and sat down across from Kara, the twelve-string guitar in his lap. Then she noticed Brian sit in the wingback chair near the stove and slip his long arms through the straps of the accordion. "God," she said. The laughter was already out before she thought to stifle it, and then trying and failing to stifle it made her laugh louder. Her mother laughed too, at Brian and at her daughter.

"Hey, they're making fun of me, Mrs. Ford," Brian said cheerfully. The old woman stared blankly at him. He squeezed the accordion in and out a few times, stopped abruptly, said, "Hey, we're honored to be playing for this union of the Husvedts and the Jo-Jokelas," and then started playing in earnest, a simple polka.

Chuck smiled knowingly and waited. Brian stopped, then banged out into four hard chords, "Bum-bam-bum-bam," that Kara suddenly recognized as the opening to "Purple Haze." He played eight more chords, faster, and

Chuck and Art joined in on the guitars, Chuck quickly flubbing his part. They stopped, laughed together.

"How's this?" Brian said. This time he muddled the song, tried again, and gave up. "Sorry. That was a little Ah-Airplane. Doesn't lend itself to, you know, a cross-over arrangement."

"Crossover?" Kara asked.

"Into the language of the accordion. My failing, I'm sure."

He took a pull off his beer and started playing again, this time something sad and sweet, Chuck and Art improvising around him.

Kara listened, slumping into her mother. "When you see a movie, and there's a scene of Paris," she asked, "why do they always play accordion music? Is there some guy with one of these on every street corner?"

"Ahh." Her mother smiled absently. "It only takes one corner, on one night, in the right month of your young life." She laughed to herself. "I hope sometime when you get a few years older you'll want to go there. You know, maybe for a few weeks. God, what am I saying?" She stroked her daughter's hair. "You won't hear me say that again. But I give you permission to mention it to me a few years from now. If you've saved some money. And you've finished at least a few years of college."

"Gee, thanks, Mom. So when I'm like twenty-one, I have your permission to discuss the possibility of going to France—if I'm paying my own way? You're the best mom in the world."

"Child, this is not the time for sarcasm."

"Sorry." She moved away from her mother. "It was a sweet thing to say."

They listened together. Even Mrs. Ford paused to take

in the sound, then rose and began clearing the dishes. Gretchen waved at her to stop, but the older woman pretended not to notice and, finally, Gretchen let her go on.

After a few more minutes, the three men reached the end of whatever they were playing. Brian cleared his throat. "OK, try this," he said. He closed his eyes and started squeezing the accordion, gently fingering the keys. Chuck just listened. "Come on," Brian urged him.

"It's been a long time. I don't think I remember it."

"Sure you do." Brian kept playing the first few bars, waiting for him. Chuck hesitated, played, botched it. Brian came around again and this time Chuck joined him in earnest; Art followed. Together they sang:

"Old man sunshine—listen, you!
Never tell me dreams come true.
Just try it and I'll start a riot.
Beatrice Fairfax, don't you dare,
Ever tell me he will care;
I'm certain it's the final curtain,
I never want to hear
from any cheerful Pollyannas,
who tell you fate supplies a mate.
It's all bananas.

"They're playing songs of love, but not for me.
A lucky star's above, but not for me.
With love to lead the way, I've found more clouds of
    gray
Than any Russian play could guarantee.
I was a fool to fall and get that way;
Hi-ho! Alas! And also, lack-a-day!

Although I can't dismiss the memory of his kiss,
I guess he's not for me."

Kara whispered to her mother: "Who is that?"
"Cole Porter, maybe. No, it's Gershwin, I think."
"How do a bunch of old hippies know Gershwin?"
Gretchen shrugged.
"It's so sad."
Art's eyes remained closed, his mouth contorted as he
sang another verse:

"I know that love's a game; I'm puzzled just the same,
Was I the moth or flame? I'm all at sea.
It all began so well, but what an end!
This is the time a feller needs a friend,
When every happy plot ends with the marriage knot,
And there's no knot for me."

They repeated the refrain. Art and Chuck played a few
chords more, stopped, and listened as Brian ended with
a flourish. Art slipped the guitar strap over his head.
"Whoa. That's great," he said. He smiled brightly. "I
could play that stuff all night."

"OK, then," Brian said. "Put on the coffee, ma-mama."

"Yeah, but that's enough. I gotta go." Art sighed
loudly and stood. "Look, any problems or anything, I'll
be around. I'll take a few of those records too, if it's OK.
I'm sort of in the mood to get hammered and listen to
Louis Prima."

Chuck said, "We don't have to keep playing. You
don't want to stay here, get hammered with us?"

"No, thanks. You guys have had a long day, heh?"

"Your call. The records are . . . you know."

Art hesitated, then pulled a dozen albums from the bottom of the bookshelf. Toward the kitchen, he yelled good night to Mrs. Ford but didn't wait for a reply. He nodded once to Gretchen and Kara, then left. Not four minutes had passed from the end of the song to his first step outside. Brian stood and slung the accordion over one arm, saying, "He's my ride." He nodded seriously and went out, shutting the door behind him.

"Oh, my," said Chuck. He played a quick riff, then gently stroked one last minor chord, a desolate sound that resonated with the wind and the distant thonking and the sound of Art's pickup rolling onto the highway.

# Jeanine

*More than what he looked like . . . or what his hair was like . . . or what he wore or said . . .*

*More than anything, I remember the couch. A big green thing, chunks of carved wood on the arms and back, thick arms where you could set down a beer and an ashtray, and they would stay there. Something from the forties that someone had found somewhere and dragged to the cabin. I remember watching him work that Indian design into the dirt floor, running his hands over the smooth rocks, me running my hand over the prickly green upholstery and feeling like this is the one. It wasn't really a romantic feeling, more a thought. More an understanding of a simple fact: This one. That part was so calming. All the sweat and all the worry and heartache and then— poof!—it's over. Now you know, honey. This one. And then that went away because I would always freeze up, and it would make me insane. I was sitting there rubbing away at a spot on the upholstery where the prickly part was already gone and thinking-thinking-thinking about what I could say to him that would make it finally happen. Take something that was inevitable and bring it to life. Because I wanted it right away. It was comforting to know that it was going to happen, but I wanted to make it real. Right then.*

*And then he was sitting beside me on the couch, and he said whatever it was and I laughed and said to him something like, "Well, I guess you don't flirt much, do you?" And he smiled because I was being just coy enough not saying yes right away. But saying yes. I can't remember what he said exactly, but it doesn't matter—it was "Let's have a kiss" or "How about a kiss?" Not "Kiss me." He wasn't that pushy. And not "I want to kiss you"—that would have been too formal for friends. We were friends, from the start, and then we became fuck-buddies. That was what he called it even though I asked him not to. Even then, "fuck-buddies" seemed awfully juvenile to me, too dopey and backslappy. Some words between a man and a woman, you should be able to just barely breathe them in the other person's ear. You can't whisper "fuck-buddy."*

*I remember the couch. I remember I had Dentyne in my mouth the first time he kissed me. When I was a kid I chewed bubble gum and then I switched to Dentyne and thought: My, how sophisticated. It was the tiny little pieces, each one wrapped in red and white.*

*I threw the gum in the fireplace and it was like I'd dropped the checkered flag in front of him. I remember his lips and tongue and his hands all over and in me and then making love with him. And everything that happened only made me think again and again: This one. This one. Jesus, please, this one.*

*I don't know how I messed it up. I was never posses-
sive. Never clingy. Some girls sleep with a guy and next
thing they're telling him what shirts not to wear and can
he reschedule his ski trip because some fat old aunt is going to be visiting from the Cities or Milwaukee.*

*I never demanded, never got sour with him. But I also
never got unfrozen in my head. I'd try to make the bridge
but it never got over there to him. What I said was stupid
or out of place and then after a while he wasn't listening.
I tried to make up for being brain-paralyzed. I tried to
make sure that all the rest of me moved for him.*

*A guy sleeps with you and ignores you and sleeps with
you again. And ignores you again. You let yourself not
care and hope that your brain will kick in and you'll be
able to make him laugh. Make him sit back and say,
"That's interesting." But then he dumps you, and takes
up with a girl who's always been a bitch to you, and you
try to rise above it. You sleep with him anyway, to get
back at her and him and because you're always thinking
that nothing is forever. And then when she proves it and
dies, does he come back to you? No. He hits the road.
You get one postcard from Africa, from fucking Chad, because of some dumb joke you'd had about a TV actor.
You get one postcard and a story every other year from
Leo or Art. And then nothing.*

*A woman could be bitter but I wasn't. I remembered
how strong the feeling was then. It was a sure thing. My
sure thing and his. Even though it was half a life ago, I
always think of him then as being him today and me as
me. It's a trick of memory, OK, but more than that. Because something about each of us hasn't changed since
then. We have souls, and when the souls are matched it
doesn't matter what happens to the bodies or the minds*

*that feed off those souls. The part that linked us then still links us. I am a middle-aged woman now and I still feel the touch of a boy's hands. The touch doesn't burn. It exhilarates me. Makes me tremble. Makes me open up.*

*Touch me. Touch me. I look at the letters in the word and they are so amazingly right. Touch. The hard bars . . . the perfect circle . . . and after that everything is opened in every possible way. Split open? Or maybe just receptive. It doesn't matter to me.*

*My memory lies all the time, but not about this. I saw him, and got that trembling, queasy, hot shivering again. It steals the will. You cry for more. And it meant something. The soul has to speak through the body . . . it doesn't have a voice of its own.*

*I remember the feeling from twenty years ago and it is unmistakable. How many times in life can you say that? He was my sure thing. And I still thought it was a sure thing when I saw him in the bar. But it was different at the reading. Just the three of them. For the first time it wasn't so clear to me. Maybe the soul does age and change. Maybe he is not my sure thing anymore. But I am his.*

*I am a middle-aged woman now. I have my poor wrecked husband and my rich fat lover. Everything is different now but his love still rules me. Could anything be more miraculous? More pathetic?*

# Nine

## 11:45 P.M.

She was floating not on but in. Cutting lazy, weightless rolls in the cosmos. Cold in the way that does not chill the body but numbs it, sapping all sense. The air, already dusty, was growing slowly more opaque: a trashy red-pink gas the color of cotton candy, with long fibrous particles that danced between her and the stars, that filled her mouth and lungs with soot. She gagged. She clawed at the thickening vapors.

Suddenly, the scent of tobacco. Not the heavy smell of someone smoking at a party or in a car, when the odor soaked into her skin, her hair, her clothes. No: this was a bright point of aroma, as though a single hard drop of the essence of tobacco had been placed on the rim of her nostril. She could feel the wetness and the repellent acridity and she jerked away, streaking into consciousness.

Kára woke up, the tobacco smell still around her in

the real world, but quickly passing. The thonk sounded again—a loose window, perhaps, a shutter being wrestled by the storm outside.

She was surprised to be awake. She had been up late talking with Mrs. Ford and Chuck and her mom, one of those long, stilted conversations that made you wish people played bridge more often. Or that there had been a TV in the house. Or that she liked to read. She'd watched the fire through the slits in the old wood stove and paged through *Elle* magazine, listening to Chuck try to convince Mrs. Ford to give him the diary.

When she could take it no longer, she went to her room. She was going to wear a nightgown, but the sheets were so cold they felt wet. So she got out of bed and put on the ugly half-poly sweat clothes her mother had made her buy at the Price Club.

A half hour after she'd gone to bed, she'd heard Chuck and her mom come up. In a few seconds they were into it with both feet—not a fight but an episode. Gnashing of garments, rending of teeth. Nothing new there: her father, Billy, had been a master of major adult anguish. It baffled her how adults took such pride in their emotional excesses, while her friends—their children—were so withdrawn, so humiliated by such behavior.

For her father it had been more than a simple lack of emotional discipline. It was—so he said—her mother. And his weakness: he was giving too much. To save his soul, to find his true Billy-ness, to achieve his destiny, yada-yada-yada, he had left them. He had run away with the best, most life-affirming rationale. But he had run away. She wasn't going to write him off but she wasn't going to respect him, either.

You are loyal to those who are loyal to you, she thought.

She was not yet loyal to Chuck. He was decent and usually honest, but flaky. From the minute you met him you knew he was capable of vaporizing himself. Poof! and he'd be gone. Even if he wanted to hang around, she knew her mother could drive him away. And even if he wanted to stay and her mother didn't make him nuts, what was the upside? She'd wind up being loyal to Chuck and not her true father and it would make her nuts when she was in her mid-thirties.

Something to look forward to, she thought now, and then she closed her eyes and could sense the heaving of the ferry on the water. She was tired, but with the weird tobacco smell caroming around the bedroom, she craved a cigarette. She found her purse in the dark, plucked out the cigarettes and lighter and took them to the window near her bed. She cracked it so that a frigid gush of air slipped in, chilling her through her sweatshirt and sweatpants. That and the recurring thonking and the dancing of the branches outside her window and the thrashing waves on the ramshackle pier all made her ache for something more comforting than a cigarette.

She decided to go downstairs, and smoke in the warm comfort of the living room, and read one of the old, frayed *Vogue*s that her mother had brought along.

She moved quietly out of her room and down the hall, so as not to disturb Chuck and her mother. They had left a light on downstairs, so it was easy to find her way. But as she reached the end of the hall, she heard a faint click, the sound of a glass being set on the hard marble of the living-room end table. She paused. The scent of tobacco was drifting from downstairs. Someone was drinking and having a cigarette. A chill spread away from the base of her neck, raising the downy hairs on her shoulders.

She moved cautiously toward the banister, then noiselessly down the next step. And the next. There she squatted, pushing her long hair out of her face, and saw one of Mrs. Ford's round and tired arms and the top of her gray head. The door to the wood stove was open and she was sitting in the old wingback chair, staring at the embers. On the end table lay an ashtray and a small juice glass and a bottle of brownish liquor. A faint halo of smoke floated between her and the small reading lamp.

The old woman made no movement and for a moment Kara was afraid that she had fallen asleep while smoking. She waited. She waited. Finally, Mrs. Ford sighed, and her unseen arm rustled. A jet of smoke rose over the back of the chair and dissipated.

OK, she's awake, Kara thought. She steadied herself, preparing to creep back up the stairs. She paused, and in that instant the old woman's voice etched a defect in the stillness: "He was a bastard, you know."

A cold finger traced across her shoulders again—at first because she thought she had been discovered and then because she was afraid Mrs. Ford had been slandering someone to the empty night and then because—as she thought this, the blood hummed in her ears—there might be a stranger in the room, by the sliding glass doors, whom she could not see.

She froze. The gray head remained immobile for a moment, then twisted down and around the wing of the chair and stared up, her two beetle-black eyes trained on Kara. "Don't sit up there spying on me," she said in a hoarse whisper. "Come on down. Have a smoke. Chat with an old witch."

She had no choice. To turn and run would have been humiliating. And what if the old housekeeper came after her, wanted to visit in her room?

She walked quickly down the stairs, keeping her eyes trained on the deck door in case someone was standing there. They were alone. She chose the couch, pulling the orange-and-brown afghan off its back as she sat, and wrapped herself up.

Mrs. Ford took another deep drag off her cigarette—one of the ultralong, ultrathin brands—and exhaled slowly. Kara lit up and grimaced at the first taste of the tobacco.

"It's late," Kara said.

Mrs. Ford looked outside, or at the panel of glass that looked out on the deck; now it showed only the bleary reflection of the reading lamp and the chair and the room behind it. "Is it?" She kicked off a shoe and rubbed the blue-veined foot against her other calf. "Your parents went to bed and I was just sitting here."

"I guess it must be strange," Kara offered. "To be in the house with us now, instead of Chuck's dad."

"Chuck's dad was a bastard. He was a hateful man, and stupid in many ways. You could see it in his eyes. For a handsome man, he had small stupid eyes. And he didn't much like women. Didn't much like me, anyway. Didn't much like Chuck, either, which was one of the few things Chuck and I had in common. We both wanted Leo to like us. And he wouldn't."

At first, Kara took this to be a confession that the old woman had been a lover, or common-law wife, or whatever they would call it up here. Then she was not so sure.

"Chuck's told you all the stories about Leo, I'm sure." She snubbed out her cigarette. "That's why I was surprised he came up here. Surprised he wanted anything to do with the old man, or this house, or this island. They almost killed your dad, you know?"

"Chuck isn't my dad," Kara said, abruptly. She said it vehemently, because it was true and because it had been the first thing she had been able to say to the old woman. It was a way to stake out conversational territory. "My father's in Alaska."

"He had another wife, you know. Chuck did. Little Mary Nordquist." Here the black eyes shot up at her, boozy but still penetrating. "She was a wild one, not like your mother. Wicked. Well, maybe not wicked. Not strong enough to be good around the people who were around her. Maybe that's it."

Kara pulled hard on the cigarette, liking the way it burned down into her lungs, and tried to match the old woman's stare.

Mrs. Ford sipped her whiskey. "Leaving was the smartest thing your father ever did. Not that he had any choice. They almost killed him after Mary died, you know. She got drunk and drove through the ice, but some of them said he'd drowned her. She was well liked, for all her nastiness."

Kara coughed as she exhaled and it made her throat feel raw. "Chuck? Come on." She knew that she was hugely ignorant about the world, but she thought she had a handle on the people in her orbit who were most likely to commit murder. A couple of boys at school. That droopy-eyed Holmgren girl who worked at Burger King. But Chuck? Who wouldn't look her boyfriends in the eye, who wouldn't drive over sixty miles an hour, who had been too scared to ride that beautiful sky-blue Triumph?

"You laugh now."

"I wasn't laughing." In fact, the rasp in her throat made it hard to talk. She coughed again.

"Here." Mrs. Ford handed her the whiskey glass and Kara drank. The fumes filled her sinuses and she thought she would gag. But the liquor was surprisingly smooth, and it eased the scratch deep in her throat.

Mrs. Ford looked away, toward the glass doors and the unseen lake beyond them. "You look at him now, and he's older. A little slower. But he was a wild one in his day. Not like the other boys. I was never one of the ones that said he was crazy, and if he did get rid of little Mary Nordquist that only proves I was right." Kara rubbed out the cigarette and sat back, light-headed. "Leo was the crazy, if you get down to it."

"I'm sorry, I have to go back upstairs now," Kara said. She felt suddenly exhausted and a little nauseous.

The old woman looked startled, as if she'd been talking to someone else and been cut off abruptly. "Sure. You run along. But I have some things you'll want to see. Things of Leo's that you should take back with you when you leave."

Kara started to stand. "That's Chuck's department, I think."

"Run along now. I'll show you tomorrow. Not everything . . ." Here she smirked, and tapped the spine of a book wedged between the chair arm and her thigh. "But plenty."

"What's the book?"

She quickly put her hand over the spine. "Nothing."

Kara wondered if liquor was enough to explain the old woman's behavior. "Yes, well, that will be nice." She pulled her hair out of her face and tried to smile. "You're OK here, then? I mean, do you need anything . . . ?"

"Will I be all right here, child? Ha. Yes, I imagine I can make do on that couch. Or the kitchen floor. I can make do."

"Someone could give you a ride somewhere."

"A ride?" She squirmed a little in the high chair, her face puckered into a tight smile, and for an instant it seemed as if her eyes were rolling back into her head. "You go on."

Kara left quickly, her light-headedness now transformed into speed. In what seemed like an instant she was up the stairs and past the room where her mother and Chuck were sleeping. No light filtered under the door. Her mind was working feverishly—already she was phrasing how she would tell all this to her mother and to Chuck. To her mother, at least. Yes, first to her mother. She was in her room with the door shut securely and she was in her bed. She was feeling light-headed again and weak and the wind seemed to be moving the house and her body ached as if it were previewing a case of the flu and she was not tired.

# Ten

## 12:15 A.M.

Tired like this she could sleep through the storm and the rattle of the shutters in a distant part of the house and the cold draft seeping through the window frame near her bed. But the soft rustle of her daughter moving down the hall roused her at once. It was Kara's pace or her pheromones or a mother's psychic antennae—whatever it was cleared her head, pulled it off the pillow. She swung her sweat-suited legs out from under the quilt, trying not to jostle the open springs and wake Chuck. She turned to pull the faded quilt up over his shoulder and realized he was not there.

The room suddenly felt chillier. She moved quickly out the door, down the wood-planked hallway.

She knocked softly on Kara's door, opened it a crack, said, "Hi," and let herself in. If her daughter had been just two years younger, she would have edged her over in the bed and slid in beside her, under the heavy pile of covers, and they would have enjoyed playing sisters.

Tonight she crouched beside the bed, feet on the cold floor. "What's up?" she whispered. "Can't sleep?" She could smell the cigarette but said nothing.

"Yeah." Kara had her large eyes, and Gretchen could see—even in the dark—that they were open and troubled. "I went downstairs and had to talk to Mrs. Ford, who's completely loopy."

"I know. Is she drunk too?"

"I can't tell what's alcohol and what's craziness. But, Mom . . . I think she's got the diary. She had it tucked right beside her in the chair."

Gretchen's voice slid out of a whisper: "Did Chuck see it?"

"Chuck? I thought he was asleep."

"That's funny. He must have gone out." The thought of their being alone in the house was unnerving. "Or maybe he's digging through stuff in the office." She ran a hand over her daughter's hair. "You OK?"

"Sure. But I want to leave. Tomorrow. Is that possible?"

"I don't know." She touched her daughter's hair again, a gesture that comforted her at least as much as it did Kara. "I know it's been hard . . . and strange. But don't be too down on Chuck. Don't completely hate him. I think he feels bad about not telling us. I think . . . I don't know how to put this . . . but those times . . ."

"I've heard all the stories."

"And don't worry about him taking the money. OK, I'm not the best judge of character." She smiled wryly at her daughter, then felt awkward because the joke, after all, was that she had erred so in marrying Kara's father. "The point is, Chuck is honest. Responsible. As cute as he is, I wouldn't have married him if he wasn't. What you heard coming out of him was years of anger. If the money is here and we do find it, we'll give it back. He wants to think about keeping it, but he's not that kind of person."

"I don't know what kind of person he is," Kara said. "But I'll give him that he's probably the least creepy person who ever lived here."

A door slammed downstairs, and Kara sat up, saying, "She left. Lock the doors."

Then Gretchen heard his footsteps on the stairs. He was moving softly, trying not to disturb them. She stuck her head out of Kara's room. Silhouetted in the light from downstairs, his face was unseeable. But she could recognize the shape of his curly hair, his long fingers on the bathroom doorknob. "We're in here," she whispered loudly.

"Minute," he said. He disappeared and water began humming in the pipes. A few moments later he joined them. Gretchen could feel the cold and wet still radiating off him.

"Was she still down there?" Kara said.

"Who? Mrs. Ford? No. I thought she went home hours ago."

"I don't know if she has a home of her own," Gretchen said. "And where were you?"

"What's that supposed to mean?"

"It doesn't mean anything. I was nervous, that's all. You could have left a note or something."

"I didn't think of it." He jammed his hands in his pockets and shivered violently, but only once. "All of a sudden, I had an idea about where Leo might have put the money. I wanted to check it out. If we don't get the diary from Mrs. Ford, I'm going to have to figure out the hiding place on my own. Anyway, I struck out."

"I saw it, I think," Kara said. "The diary. She had an old blue book with her, in the living room. Just a few minutes ago."

"What was she doing with it?"

"Nothing. She was just sitting in front of the stove and she had it beside her."

"Damn. Wait here." He ran downstairs. She heard him stop at the bottom, then dash across the floor. A few moments later, he was back. "Nothing there now. I even checked the wood stove to see if she'd tossed it in there. You're sure it was the diary?"

"No," said Kara. "But she was pretty nervous when I saw it."

"Where'd she go?" Gretchen asked.

"Who knows," he said. "She's not downstairs. She could be wandering around outside, or maybe she went back to wherever she goes when she's not here. I'm not going to try to flush her out tonight. We'll see her tomorrow and there'll be a way to convince her to hand it over. For now, I need some sleep." He glanced down at Gretchen. "You coming?"

"In a minute," she said.

The hard wet hands were under his small body, lifting him up. He tried to twist away but could not. He was fighting to get free, to be dropped if need be on the new cement but not back into the freezing suffocation of the lake. He struggled fiercely and then was up and over and then the hands were gone and for an instant he was fixed in space—free of the hands and able to breathe. Then the cold collapsed around him and he struck out kicking and pulling for the surface, trying not to open his mouth or his eyes, but panicking instantly. Opening both. Sucking in water and blinding his eyes. Then the hard steel of the pole clubbed into his arm, the side of his head. He reached for it and climbed with all the adrenaline-fired power his young body could churn out. He was out, breathing mostly air now, and his father's powerful arms were pulling him down the pier. When he tried to reach for the sides, the pole pushed him farther away. "Swim for it!" his father roared. "Go on! Swim!"

His eyes snapped open and he was awake, staring at the charcoal-dark ceiling. No jumping or flinching. Just open, awake. End of dream.

That, he thought, is getting off easy. He sat up, swung his feet onto the floor. It was still night. The center of his belly felt hollow, but otherwise he was fine: no vestigial fear or madness. Lucky. Sometimes the dreams stuck with him, rode beside him through the day, so that he could be working on a mundane project—trying to figure out how to squeeze out an extra six inches of kitchen counter space, where to vent a range hood—and be overcome with sadness and dread. This time, it didn't stick. Lucky.

Then he heard the voices yelling downstairs. He rubbed his face and stood, thinking Gretchen and Kara must be going at it in the kitchen. He felt guilty, knowing he was the root cause for every bad thing that happened to them up here. Then he realized suddenly that a third voice was taking part.

He sprinted down the stairs, the actions still grooved even though he had last executed this pattern of leaps and handholds two decades before. As he pivoted around the newel post, he saw Mrs. Ford. She was weaving, pointing violently at Gretchen.

". . . what anybody . . ." Here she labored for breath, failed to fill her lungs, but rushed on anyway: ". . . or any government institution . . . or snoopy people"—gasp— "and I mean *you* snoopy people. *You* people are going to pay for what happened here. And what *didn't* happen."

"What the hell is going on?" he demanded.

"We came down for some tea," Gretchen snapped. "She suddenly appeared at the door and walked in here and started threatening us."

"Threatening?" He looked at Mrs. Ford.

The old woman swallowed two deep breaths before speaking. "I only said that she had better be careful. That's all. A warning is not a threat, young lady." She looked not at Gretchen this time but at Kara, who was sitting at the kitchen table, her cheek cupped in an open hand. Kara rolled her eyes.

Suddenly the old woman's yellowed eyes moved past Kara to the kitchen counter, and a look of sharp fear crossed her face. She inched forward, then reached the counter in a fast shuffle of her feet. Chuck saw the worn blue book in the same instant that her leathery fingers snatched it up.

"What is that?" he asked.

"Something of mine," she screeched.

"That's it, isn't it?" Chuck said, his voice more exasperated than angry. "That's his diary." He lowered his voice. "I don't want to keep it, OK? But we have to go over everything. To figure out the estate."

"That's just what they want, isn't it? All his records to come out." She backed up a step, until she was leaning against the counter by the sink.

"No one needs to see it but me, Mrs. Ford. And I'll treat everything in there with absolute confidence. Believe me. There's probably some stuff about me in there that I don't want broadcast."

"You know there is. I'd be doing you a favor destroying this, mister. But that's not why I'll do it. I don't much care about your troubles. I care about Leo's name. No one's going to tear him apart now that he's gone. That's why no one gets to see this. No one." Mrs. Ford held it tight to her chest. "It must disappear."

He took a small step toward her and stopped. "But you understand that it's mine now. Leo left it to me, Mrs. Ford. If you'd been at the reading, you'd know that. Legally, it belongs to me."

"Ha!" She crept sideways against the counters, away from him. "I love getting legal advice from any man in this house."

"It probably has information that I need. Desperately."

She stepped closer to the door. "You can be sure that it does have information but it's nothing that concerns you. You weren't interested in what he could give you when he was alive. Now it's too late to go digging through his private thoughts. You have no right."

"I don't want to take it from you."

"Ahh!" She lurched toward the sink, jerking a steak knife out of the dish drainer. It was not a big knife, and she was in no condition to defend herself if he decided to take the diary away from her. Still, he hesitated. Put together any drunk and any knife and anyone could get hurt.

"OK, OK. Just put the knife down. Gretchen, move. Get behind me. Kara . . ." Getting up from the table and moving around it would bring her too close to the distraught housekeeper. "Kara, stay there. Look ... Mrs. Ford ... I give up. You can have the damn book. I'll help you burn it."

"No you don't. You'll stay right where you are. Move and I'll kill you."

"Lord, what the hell is in there?" He said it out loud, then wished he hadn't.

"That is something you will never find out. Not you. Not the government. Not those people in town. Not anyone." Still holding the knife up, she crept toward the back door. She opened it with a quick wrench, scuttled out, never turning her back on them, never lowering the knife. Behind her, the clouds had blown off and a brilliant moon reflected off the lake.

Chuck spread his arms, trying to calm her, but she screamed at him and pivoted, her shoes slapping down the wooden stairs to the beach.

He ran to the door, called out to her. Every time he called her name she seemed to jerk a little, run a little faster. He started down the steps, after her.

"Stop," Gretchen called to him. "Let her go."

"She's out of her head," he said. "She's going to hurt herself."

"I don't care. Let her go. She's got a knife, Chuck."

"Don't worry," he yelled back. "I can take care of her."

# Eleven

Her mother was on the landing, yelling at Chuck. "Let her go! I don't care about it! Who needs it?"

But Chuck was gone. From the kitchen window, Kara could see two shapes running in the moonlight. The first one stopped, tried to run again. Stumbled and went down, the wind tugging at her housedress. Then, as Chuck approached, she scrambled to her feet and ran down the crumbling pier. Chuck hesitated, then stooped over and followed, crawling hand over hand on the out-thrust jumble of rocks and concrete.

"Mom," she cried. "He's following her out on the pier. He's going to freak out there." Gretchen moved toward the back door but Kara screamed at her. "Don't leave me here alone. I'm coming too."

"No. I don't want you out there."

"I'm not waiting up here alone."

106

"You'll stay, even if it means I have to stay with you." She put a tensed hand on her daughter's shoulder and stopped her sharply. "You are not going to be part of this."

Her mother stood beside her now at the window. They stared until Chuck and Mrs. Ford got about midway down the pier, where their view was blocked by a big maple. Kara said, "I've lost them. They're out on the pier but the tree's in the way."

"He can't go out on the pier," her mother moaned. "He'll fall to pieces. He won't be able to protect himself from her."

"We can see them from the deck."

Before her mother could respond, Kara sprinted to the living room, then out onto the deck. The temperature had plummeted since she'd come in before supper, and the cold shocked her. He's not wearing any shoes, she realized.

She could hear nothing over the beat of the waves and the rustle of the wind-tossed maple. Through its limbs, she could make out the last twenty feet of the pier below. One silhouette crouched at the tip of the rubble.

Her mother came out behind her. "Where is he?" she asked urgently.

"There." Kara pointed at the dark figure. Then, for an instant, it stood upright and she was sure it was Mrs. Ford. "Oh, God." She shuddered. But when the figure bent low again, and began to crab its way back to solid ground, she knew it was him. She watched, frozen, until the stooped figure was obscured again by the tree.

"He got off," she said. "He's coming back."

"Where is she?" Gretchen demanded. "Where's Mrs. Ford?"

"I don't know. He's alone, I think."

Gretchen stared down at her.

"Maybe she fell in," Kara said. "I mean, they both went out there and now he's coming back by himself."

"Oh, Jesus." Her mother dashed off the deck, and Kara followed her—into the house, out to the back landing. Her mother yelled, "Chuck? Chuck?" as she ran. As they reached the landing, the breeze shook a thin volley of raindrops out of the trees, chilling Kara even more. Now she watched her mother clamber down the stairs and she was afraid suddenly that the shadowy form trudging across the beach toward them was neither Chuck nor Mrs. Ford but someone else.

Her mother recognized him first. She called his name and scrambled down the remaining stairs. He took her embrace, then kept coming, an arm around her waist. From the landing, Kara yelled down to him, "Where is she?" He shook his head and kept climbing the stairs. "Where is Mrs. Ford?" He passed her without looking or speaking.

Back in the kitchen, he dropped into one of the straight-back chairs, tossing the blue diary onto the table. He was drenched. His sweatpants were sodden up to his knees. The front of his sweatshirt was molded to his body, as if he'd been hit by a heavy wave spray.

"I lost her," he said simply. He looked into Gretchen's eyes for a moment, then down. "She was screaming at me to stop, so I stopped. I did, I stopped. But she kept going. When she went off the end I tried to catch her but I couldn't reach her. She just went in and then . . ."

"She's still in the water?"

Kara ran for the door, but he screamed, "Wait!" and caught her arm. He held on and her own force swung her around, and when she slipped she crashed hard on the kitchen floor.

"It's over," he growled. "I won't have you killed out there too."

She screamed at him to let go and he did, but he swore at her: "God damn it, Kara. You go out there and you risk killing yourself. She went straight down. Didn't come up again. I don't know what happened." He stared at them both, pleading. "She might have slipped on some ice. Or it might have been on purpose. She was insane out there."

Kara pulled herself up into a crouch. Her head ached. "How did you get that?" she demanded, pointing at the notebook. Her voice shook.

"I picked it up off the pier." He stared at it blankly. "She must have dropped it when she started to fall."

Kara was stunned. "You couldn't save her but you could get the damn notebook?"

Her mother hissed: "Kara!"

"She fell in the water," he said, pleading again. "This didn't. I tried to get her but I couldn't." He bent his head into his right hand and sobbed. "I tried and tried but I couldn't do it. I couldn't go into the water. I couldn't reach her."

Her mother kneeled before him. "Chuck. You did what you could. She was half nuts and drunk. She had a knife. She was going to stab you. Us."

"We have to do something," Kara insisted.

"Yes, of course," he said. His eyes were vacant now. He stared through the kitchen wall down to the beach. "I have to find her. If I don't find the body, God knows where she's going to wash up."

"You sit here, Chuck," Gretchen said soothingly.

"You're wet. You've been through enough. I'll call Lyle and Art and they can come out and find her."

"Are you crazy?" He stood up woodenly, knocking the chair backward. Kara jerked herself away. He looked crazy to her. She looked instinctively for something to use against him. Something with a handle. She hadn't really hit anyone since childhood, but she had seen it done, and not just in movies. What she'd seen had sickened her, but it taught her a lesson. People could be dropped. Quickly. There was nothing within reach, though, and she was afraid of spooking him even more.

"You stay right here and don't you dare call the cops. Don't you dare." He looked at the phone and—Kara could see it—he was thinking about tearing it out of the wall. He stopped himself. "You should be trying to *help* me. The cops! This is all they need. They'll have my ass in jail like nothing."

Her mother stared at him, bewildered.

"What are you going to do?" Gretchen asked finally. "*Not* tell them? How long before they find her and put together a story that's much worse than the truth? I know you're a little rattled now, but you have to see that. You have to tell them."

"You're wrong there, Gretchen. Lots of things happen in a place like this and they never get figured out." He stripped off his soaked shirt and grabbed a heavy windbreaker off a hook by the back door. He threw it on over his naked chest. He reached for a pair of weathered Sorels by the back door and pulled them on over his bare feet. "People disappear. After a while, they come back. Or they don't. Things go on." He zipped up the jacket and grabbed a flashlight off the counter. "You think only city people get away with shit?"

He was out the back door. Gretchen followed him, wordlessly, to the landing but not down the stairs. She watched the back of the windbreaker shine faintly in the moonlight as he crossed the beach. She turned, then, and went to the phone. She lifted the receiver.

# Twelve

## 1:30 A.M.

When Gretchen woke up she thought she'd been asleep for several hours. Her right arm was prickly, almost numb, and a thin crust had formed in the corner of one eye. But there was only a subtle change in the light: outside the deck's plate-glass doors, the sky was still black, but clouds had fallen over the moon again. She looked at her watch and saw that just twenty minutes had passed. Her head felt strange—at once stuffed and light.

Kara was slumped beside her on the couch, under the brown-and-orange afghan. Her breathing was rough and loud, which could have been a bad cold and could have been her asthma kicking in. Name three splendid ways to set off an asthma attack, Gretchen thought: emotional stress, physical stress, an old dusty house. And you are doing nothing about her smoking. You could, but you don't have the strength anymore.

She closed her eyes for an instant and thought: Lazy. You're a giving parent, but so lazy.

She hadn't called Lyle, but it was not out of laziness. It had taken great strength to put the phone back in its cradle and meet her daughter's eyes. She'd tried to explain to Kara, but the longer she talked, the thinner her reasoning became. Kara had pressed her, asking how she could continue to trust him, how she could allow herself to be drawn into something that was so clearly wrong. Something that invited so much trouble.

She didn't budge. It was part trust in his judgment, she said. Part loyalty. And though she did not include this, it was also part momentum: Once you have made the first step, a crime spins its own degenerate logic. And she did not delude herself: It was a crime.

Was it the money? Kara had asked.

No, it was not. She had been adamant. She wouldn't do this for money, for a house, for anything in the material world. Neither would Chuck. They didn't even know for sure that there *was* money.

After some minutes, Kara had quit pressing. Gretchen wondered if her daughter had really been demanding righteousness, or if it was simply a way for her to probe this adult behavior. Then she worried that Kara had stopped pressing too soon, had been too willing to yield to something so fearfully corrupt.

In their arguing, they'd moved from the kitchen to the living room, Kara falling onto one end of the couch, Gretchen onto the other. At the end of their talking, Kara had crossed her arms, slid close to her mother, and closed her eyes. Blindly, she reached out for the afghan and pulled it up around her shoulders. In an instant, it seemed, she was asleep.

Gretchen picked up the diary then. She tried to read it but lost interest, or lost the train of events where the ink was water-smeared. In the early pages, there was not much to help her decipher the man. And clearly nothing to explain why Mrs. Ford had reacted so strongly. She had dropped off thinking of the old woman. Waking now, she realized the diary had left a wet spot on her lap. She thought again of Mrs. Ford, and how pitiful it was to have died protecting a book so dreary that it lulled you to sleep even as it moistened you.

She skipped a few pages and began reading again. These early entries were devoted to Leo's political musings. The writing had a stiff quality to it, as though he was preparing a formal declaration. Something that others, coming after him, would read. You arrogant hillbilly philosopher, she thought, utterly sure of her assessment. She sniffed at whole paragraphs attributed to Ricardo and Marx, with Leo's solemn responses. There were other references—to Mao and even Nkrumah—but these seemed borrowed, even stiffer than the others.

I would have loved to have you in class, she thought. I'd have cut you off at the knees.

Gradually, the entries became more closely tied to current events. Instead of railing against abstract crimes by vague forces, Leo named transgressors and their offenses. Sinners and sins; times and places. The Israeli invasion of Lebanon got three pages. The fall of governments in Latin America warranted a paragraph here, several pages there, depending on how closely they were tied to the various cabals of Jews, Rockefellers, Trilateralists.

If for different reasons we both hated Kissinger, she wondered, is it a sign of something? Is it a good sign?

Oblique personal references were made, but infrequently. In an April 1983 entry, Leo had boasted about how much he had done for his son, how he'd tried to teach him to swim but the boy "couldn't cut it." There was more, but she was so outraged she turned the page.

Then this, from October 1983:

Of course she was weak. That much should have been expected from a woman who had been pampered so many ways by so many. But she should not have been weak with me. It could only lead to chaos. We knew that. She knew it better than me, I think, even though she was just a child.

And after she was weak with me she should have kept her own counsel. If she had mustered even the thinnest ration of discipline—if she had just shut up—nothing would have happened.

Oh God, that is foolish. And you would say wicked if you still had a conscience. For a man of God to wish that she had lied, and to call that lying discipline, is a travesty. She should not have lied, never, even to save her life. But it was wrong to tell him in that way, to use the telling as a weapon against him. She should have said it not in anger but in love, but her anger made her weak with him.

She should have known not to be weak with other men after she had been weak with me.

The entry ended. Gretchen flipped back a page, then another, then forward, but there was no other reference to whoever she was. No names were needed, Gretchen figured: Leo was talking to himself here. This was the first glimmer of intimacy between the old man and himself and she felt inexplicably happy for him. It was the same feeling she got when one of her students made a break-through. Then she tried to put a name to the woman of the entry, but the only names she had were Chuck's mother and Mrs. Ford. Then: Jeanine the bartender. Mary Nordquist.

Abruptly, a long comparison of firearms leaped out at her. She knew of Uzis from TV. She had not heard of the Mini-14 and was not sure, in fact, that it was a gun until she had read a full paragraph.

Leo's ranting continued: frothing diatribes against the Internal Revenue Service, convoluted explanations of something he called the Gold Imperative. Black-white intermarriage was evidently a problem. Matching Asians and whites was also frowned upon. Gretchen wondered if Leo would have railed against black-Asian crossbreeding. And, OK, if he did, would an East Indian–Chinese union be acceptable? How about African blacks and Melanesians?

It was at once complicated and stupid. You have been failed by your teachers, she thought. In school and out.

She closed the book, listened for Chuck, heard nothing. Only a thonking sound—a loose window, she figured—and the shifting of small branches as the stove fire burned out. The wind.

You could have gone with him, she chastised herself. You could have helped him with this hideous job.

No, you couldn't, she countered. If you had seen her, you would have lost it. You would have screamed, cried. You would have hated him. You would have insisted that he tell the deputy. Or you would have told Lyle yourself. And you would not have left your daughter to do any of it.

This is his crime, she thought. Don't let yourself be poisoned by it.

Or by this, she added, looking down at the diary. This is poison for our eyes. Twisted and prurient, like pornography.

But like the best pornography, it had just enough truth in it to engage her curiosity, to seduce her, to promise a one-way window on private realms. She opened the book again.

To her relief, there was nothing truly frightening for the rest of 1983. Nineteen eighty-four brought month after month of Leo's tedious political exegesis. His writing, which was crabbed at the beginning, grew even smaller and tighter. She jumped ahead, searching for something about Leo's finances. Just then she stumbled onto another reference to *her*. Gretchen knew, immediately, it was the same woman.

I am confused again about how these things happened with her. About how a man of dignity and intelligence and backbone can be handled so effortlessly. I have sinned before God and the Gods of my own creation. I have sinned before myself but I am a bad God, a flawed God, because I cannot forgive my own sins. And she cannot, being gone.

She ran through the names again, this time of those who were gone in 1984: Chuck's mother. Mary Nordquist.

This is bad logic, Gretchen, she told herself. You don't draw conclusions based on two days of knowing this place. She felt the chill run through her but repeated to herself: You don't draw conclusions.

The fire was nearly out in the wood stove and she was cold. Beside her, Kara's breathing was less labored. She tipped her head to rest on her daughter's, thinking: How is it that you aren't having nightmares, little one?

She slammed the book shut, opening it again immediately because in the last instant her husband's name had risen out of the tangle of the old man's script. It struck her that she had not seen his name before.

Chuck has been good in his way. He is no weakling. There are bridges burned between us. Huge spans . . . never be crossed again. But he's no stranger to action or to thought. I can respect him for that, and can rely on him, even though he does not now realize it. When the time comes, he will be ready. We are part of the same organism. This, I think, he does realize.

It is all in the breeding.

No, old man, she thought. That's cheap comfort. It's not that simple and you know it. He is no stranger to thought or action, but there is nothing of your breeding left in him. You think he's a head case and a drifter. A loser. But he's not. When he decides that something or someone is true, he sticks to it like grim death.

He is the most faithful man I know, she realized suddenly.

She shut the book, but marked the page first. She set it carefully on the end table. She put her hand on her daughter's shoulder, lightly, and envied her sleep.

# Brian

*She liked me. Some guys would have let it slip by them. Not me. I have extra senses. Extra organs.*

She liked me. So what? Here's what. Guys chase around so much other donkey shit and all they want really is to have a woman like them. Or a girl.

OK, then they want the girl to fuck them. Or give them money or something else. Like when I went to Chicago that time, I saw this black guy walk up to this pretty black girl in a bar and he looked her up and down and smiled real nice and said, "Hey. You gotta job?" So he probably wanted to get her money . . . and fuck her . . . but just because it's a way to prove to himself that she liked him. And probably because then he wouldn't have to work. And that would give him time to go find another woman to like him.

Why? Short answer: It feels good. Big rush rush rush rush ruuuuush. Epilepsy of pleasure, and not just sex but still physical. Like jogging. Maybe it makes endorphins.

*It's not my job to know. But you see it all the time in men and women. Young ones. Old ones, even as old as Leo. He was an owly old guy most of the time. Never gave off much energy. He'd move around a lot, but it always seemed fakey to me. Flat. Like he was a hologram: If you moved your head, you got the idea he was three-dimensional. If you just stood there, you got some impression of depth, but there wasn't much to grab on to. But then some young woman would come into the room and he'd get the love-rush going. He'd sit up strong and his chest would fill out. He'd inflate, like his whole body had a boner.*

*If love turns you from a hologram to a boner, you'd be pretty sold on it, wouldn't you?*

*Why? Long answer: It is a mystery. I think about it sometimes but it is beyond understanding. So let it go. Instead, I let the world funnel into me through my organs. I roll the world around in my mouth like strawberry ice milk.*

*People up here don't like black people much. I don't say much about it because as soon as I offer an opinion they say, "Shut up, you idiot." Or (if they're talkative), "Well, how many black people do you know?" And I say, "Shit, how many white people do I know?"*

*It's always an argument, so: away, away troubling talk. I let it go. But blacks are OK by me. Older ones, anyway. Funny. I know they aren't all funny and they'd be pissed off if you said to them, "You guys are a funny people," but I don't know why. Everyone always tells the German people they're tight-assed, fat, and hostile. Funny sounds OK compared to that, doesn't it?*

*So?*

*It's hard to figure.*

*So anyway I suppose I'm mostly full of crap here. I don't know what other people think or want. Don't know much about history . . . biology . . . But for Brian, it's fine to say: A very tasty sixteen-year-old girl thought I was decent. She liked talking. She liked the music.*

*It's different music than it used to be. We used to play hard rock 'n' roll—the kind guys like to listen to in weight rooms. Stuff to make your veins pop. We played decent. I swear there were nights you could smell the solder melting in the amps. Glory days, says Bruce. Stink of sweat and many smokes, beer and pee and vaporized lead solder. Don't do that no more. Mama don't allow no un-un-un around here.*

*Who's this Mama? I don't know. My personal mom is gone now. But there's a lot you aren't supposed to do anymore when you get older. There's a new Mama, new rules. No one knows who she is or where she is, but she's around. Ragging on you. I wish I could let her go, but I can't.*

*The mom didn't like me. Got that nervous look when I moved close to the girl. Henny-penny, watching her chick. (OK by me. No harm done. Predictable.) I want to say, "Hey. I am the most gentle person you've ever met." She wouldn't believe it. She'd still be a henny-penny. And that's good. You want moms to watch over their girls. I've known wayward girls, and they aren't pretty.*

*Mary, Jeanine, others. A few others. Pretty and yet not.*

*What makes some of them sad and scary? (Alone?) It's hard to figure. I know how it can happen to boys. But girls, they have a special grace, and when they lose it, they are more troubling than troubled boys.*

*You feel like you really need to do something about it. But what? You could spend your life thinking about that, but it wouldn't get you very far. So don't think about it. Just do what you do. Brian, he's OK. I know how to let go. More than any of them, with all that they have and all that they know and all that's ahead of them, I, Brian, know how to let go.*

# Thirteen

## 2:00 A.M.

He had been out there for how long—he did not know—
chilled in the windbreaker and no shirt—so stupid, so
fucking stupid—when he saw it lying there, rocked by
the waves, looking already bloated, though he knew that
could not be. She was in the shallows, sheltered from the
heavy water in a small half-circle of rock and beach, the
subdued waves still acting on her, pulling a little, pushing
a little, so she might have been still just a tiny bit alive,
still struggling for breath. But she was not. Clearly. She
was dead meat.

And damn you for it, you stupid old bitch, he thought.

He did not want to turn the flashlight on her. There was
nothing he wanted to see and he was afraid that even
here, tonight, someone would be drawn to the flicker. Especially here tonight.

They will be watching now, he thought. They will

guess when she doesn't show up somewhere, and then someone will say, well, of course, she was living in the same house with that crazy bastard, Leo's boy, and that's why none of us will see her again. And then they will come. Looking for the money, for Mrs. Ford, for Mary Nordquist. They will keep coming and coming until they think they have it all taken care of. Until he began to say things just so that they would not hound him anymore.

But he was not giving in now. He had this job to do, these people to protect. He jammed the flashlight into the pocket of the windbreaker and bent down to pull her up to dry land.

He set his teeth hard against his lip, planted his feet in the wet sand, and let the waves run over them. And he reached. He missed and reached again, the center of his gravity shifting out over the water, and he stretched out farther and still could not get her. Now the fear surged through him—the fear of the water, the fear that the waves would pull her back out, or would leave her in deep water just a few yards offshore, where he could not get to her. The lake might hold her there, in the open. And there would be nothing he could do until they found her and came for him.

He roared and took a stuttering step forward, the water over his feet now, circling his ankles and pulling, pouring into his boots and weighing him down, and he closed his eyes and reached for her, screaming now, but missed. He took another step, the water up over his calves now, cold enough to make his heart hammer dully, and he screamed louder and wept but snagged the heavy cold cotton of her dress with his fingers. He clawed at the fabric but lost her as he twisted toward shore. The desperate clutch and spin threw him toward the beach and he collapsed there, sobbing.

She floated away a foot, then bobbed back. If she would only stay put, he thought, I could snag her with a branch. Or Leo's fishing gear.

He ran to the back of the beach and then in among the maples and birches and scrub trees, searching for a branch, finding nothing long or strong enough. Turning back, he saw that she had begun to drift out, now eight feet from shore, now ten. He cried out and dashed back to the edge of the water, then in, up to his calves, his knees, but she was so far out he didn't even bother to reach for her. His legs trembled with the cold and fear and then the rage took over. He cursed the water and roared, his body filled with the hatred of it and her, and even though he was wracked by the trembling he was now in up to his thighs and now to his waist, the bellowing a part of his breathing, his legs plodding forward. He got a corner of fabric and lunged for more, as he had lunged for the metal pole, and he got it and pulled hard and she came to him. He pumped his numb legs backward furiously, the water splashing away in low, pallid arcs. And he kept pumping even after he felt the firm slap of the sand under his boots and after she grew heavy, kept pumping until the dress ripped away in his hands and he fell back on the beach with the old woman laid out before him. Thick and frigid and speckled with fine sand in the moonlight.

He breathed heavily for a minute, then turned around and watched, in absolute silence, for a sign that someone might have been watching. Might have heard. The moon slipped behind a small bank of clouds. The waves splashed at the beach, at Mrs. Ford's bare pasty legs. Nothing moved behind him.

Now to hide her, he thought.

He would need a shovel for that. They were not going to find another waterlogged body—that would be too much. This one was going in the ground. He would drag her into the woods across the highway and bury her there, deep. So deep that the frost would not heave her up where the animals could find her. He would put her way down, and cover the violated earth with branches and brush. And they would suspect him but they would never know.

They might want to hang me for Mary, he thought, or anyone else. But I can control this one. They are not going to bust my ass over this one. And he pulled her cold, flabby, dead arm over his shoulder and her other arm over his other shoulder and humped her up high on his back, piggybacking the corpse off the beach. He held tightly to her elbows and her watery gray hair brushed the back of his neck.

He would not take her up the stairs, even though that was the easiest way up the hill. He would not have Gretchen (or, worse, Kara) see the obscenity of him hauling this moist bag of flesh. He staggered down the beach a hundred yards to where the Olsons had always kept a fishing boat chained to a tree. It was still there, as was the wide path they had cut to the highway. The ground underfoot was muddy, though, and he slipped hard once, his hand striking out for support and missing, running down the jagged bark of a tree trunk, shredding his skin. He landed with a jolt on the wet ground. She shifted on his back but he did not drop her.

Slowly, his hand burning, his feet faltering, then finally catching, he crawled up the hill. At the top, he pulled her arms tighter around his neck and stood. He waited for a moment, then pushed out of the brush, over the ditch, and onto the highway. In the same instant, he heard the whine of the truck, still a mile away but barreling toward him, and she began to fight his progress. Something—the belt on her old housedress, the hem, the skin on her leg—had snagged a branch. As he jerked forward it pulled her back off his shoulders, then suddenly released her. She seemed to leap away from him to the road's asphalt and he dropped her, even as the glow of the headlights silhouetted the low rise to his left. He twisted around, embraced the body, and, with a desperate thrust of his legs, threw it and himself into the shallow ditch. They hit and rolled and he landed first, the wet corpse sagging heavily over him. He froze there, her lips pressed slackly against his ear, and waited. The truck did not pass and he could not hear its whine.

Panic thundered through him, and at its peak, just as he moved his hand to throw the body aside and run into the forest, the pickup rushed past, tossing up a halo of brilliant light and a delicate, beaded curtain of water. And then it was gone.

He waited a moment until he was sure the driver hadn't seen him. Or her. He waited another second, in case another car might be coming. Then he quickly pulled himself out of the ditch. He left her there, walked three steps down the highway and then back again, trying to shake off the disgust. Then he shouldered the body again. He crossed the asphalt and crashed into the underbrush on the other side.

He was not going to carry her along the highway. He did not even want to carry her down a path or game trail in the woods. He wanted her dumped in a part of the forest where no one would happen upon her. He bent his head and pushed on through the low branches and underbrush, changing his thinking with every heave and lurch.

If I try to leave her here, just dump her, the animals will find her. A dog might show up with a hand at someone's back door. Or if it doesn't stay cold enough, she might smell and someone would know what it was and find her.

If I leave her here for a half hour while I go back to the house and get a shovel, maybe I won't be able to find her. Then I'll have to come back out in the daylight, when people might be looking for her. Or watching me.

Or I could come back just before dawn. Even if I couldn't find her in the dark, how far off could I be? I could wait in the woods with a shovel and probably be within a hundred feet of her. And then when it got light out I could find her fast enough and dig the hole and put her in fast.

I could have the hole already dug.

If there weren't hunters around. If I'm not fifty feet from a deer blind that I can't see in the dark.

As soon as he thought of the deer blind, he shuddered. Of course. He was across the highway from Olson's boat, a hundred feet directly into the woods; that meant he was probably standing no more than a few hundred feet from the old shack that he and Art and Donny Gromek and Mary and Jeanine had used as their hideaway. Where they had smoked their first cigarettes, their first pot. Where he had made his first mosaic. Where he had seen Mary naked for the first time.

Of course. Leave her in the shack. Get the shovel. Come back. Dig a hole fifty feet away. Cover her up, go home, steal a cigarette from Kara. Shower.

He tipped his shoulder and let her slide to the forest

floor. He waited a moment in the silence to make sure he was still alone, then pulled out the flashlight. He shined it directly ahead but could see nothing. Just the wet black tree trunks, spindly suckers clinging to their few tattered leaves. He counted five steps forward, shined the light back on the body to orient himself, then forward, this time moving it in a short arc.

Nothing. He took another five steps, shined the body, shined the trees. And another. This time, when he looked ahead, he saw the puddled surface of the path. Yes, he thought, and carefully retraced his steps. He found her quickly and dragged her toward the path and then hoisted her again to his shoulders. He knew where he was going now, knew he would be there in minutes.

From the outside, the shack had changed only a little. More crowded by underbrush. A brick cracked out of the chimney. But it had not decayed. He could see that. It had not been fixed up, but it had been built well enough so that it had not fallen apart in two decades.

He put his shoulder against the door and it opened easily. The inside was small, so that the flashlight immediately illuminated it all. The bare dirt floor, broken only by the fireplace apron, flagstones framing a primitive mosaic: smooth beach rocks tamped into place to form the head of an Indian warrior. One of his first attempts, executed during a long four days of beer and marijuana. Beyond it, in the corner, a broken chair lying on its side. A wooden box, empty, stood on end. By the door, a table. On the wall across from the door, someone had nailed a shelf. A long candle rested there, supported in a thin clump of its own red wax.

He thought to light it but stopped himself. Instead, he dragged the body inside, closed the door, and walked away.

He took the main path, the one that led back to the house, and went quickly. Because he felt that much lighter without her weight on him. Because he wanted desperately to get back here and get her in the ground.

The path moved parallel to the road now, close to the house. He could see a light on in the living room. He pushed aside a branch and was about to step over the ditch and onto the highway when he saw Lyle's silver pickup parked on the lawn by the front door.

"Jesus," he said out loud.

He ducked back into the brush and crouched there. No one seemed to move inside the cab but he could not be sure. He dashed on down the path, keeping low, past the house, past the woodshed. Down another hundred yards. Then he broke through the brush and sprinted across the blacktop. On the other side he fought his way down to the beach and jogged back to the house. He walked slowly up the stairs to the top landing and took off his mud-caked boots. Behind him, the weather was gearing up again. The waves slapped higher on the beach, the wind shrieked through the trees.

Looking through the back door, he could see them standing in the dining room. Lyle, Gretchen, Kara. OK, he thought, time to get normal. He clutched the metal handle, twisted. He slowly opened the door and, as he did, a blast of arctic air snatched it violently from his hand.

# Fourteen

## 2:15 A.M.

Kara's eyes were closed but she was not asleep anymore. She lay on the couch beside Gretchen, her cheek against the thick nap of her mother's robe, listening as she ruffled the pages of the old man's diary. With each of her mother's grunts and aspirations she wanted to lift her head, ask what it was. But even more, she did not want to know. She knew it would be riveting but ghastly, the burning house with the baby inside. She knew that she would have to look eventually. But for now, no. No, thank you.

Gradually the book dropped and her mother's breathing fell into a hoarse rattle. It made her uneasy, and that, in turn, embarrassed her. She was as adult as she ever expected to be, but she nevertheless wanted her mother awake just now. Not as a guardian, specifically. But to be attentive to matters until they were all quite safe. Another part of herself, a voice that was steely but not exactly a raw bitch, arose and overrode the whining. She relaxed.

This was bad, OK, she thought. But a lot of her life was bad and she handled that OK. To convince herself, she began to catalogue the terrors that were so normal and so daily you stopped noticing them. She had friends who had been hunted by the police or their parents, who had been chased by gangs and the solo psychos no gang would have. She knew girls who would run a razor across your jacket or your face, just to see it ruined. She knew boys who wanted to drag her into their cars or vacant lots or the wild parkland near the river. She knew boys who just stared at her. The phantoms who spent too much time in their musty bedrooms, who spoke, when they talked at all, about video games and television.

She could handle all that; she could handle her father bailing out on her; she could handle this. She was angry about it, but she could handle it.

So far.

The growl of the truck on the road's gravel shoulder made her heart wallop and brought tiny beads of fear sweat to her face and arms. She jerked up, pushed her mother sharply.

"Someone's here."

Gretchen tensed even before her eyes opened. "Who is it?" she asked, but she didn't wait for an answer. She stood up, a little shaky on her feet, and brushed her hair with her hands. She looked around blankly.

"God in heaven," Gretchen said. Kara watched as it all began to seep back into her mother's consciousness. "God. What time is it?"

"A little after two."

"Where's Chuck?" her mother demanded, her voice sounding at once frightened and irritable.

"I don't know. Still outside."

"The book." Her mother snapped her fingers, pointing at the diary. "Put that under the couch." She waited a beat, then said, "Quick. Go find him. Now." And in the next instant: "Wait. Wait. No, I don't want you out there alone. You stay."

She coughed once, tossed the dark copper bangs out of her face, and went to the door. Kara thought she might be going outside, and leaped from the couch to be with her. But her mother stopped in the doorway, looked out the small diamond-shaped window, opened the door a crack. A voice spoke and her mother said, "OK. Sure. Come in."

The first person through the door, bending a little under the low frame, was Lyle Pointer. His face—as he nodded to Kara—was somber but open. I hate it when cops act like morticians, she thought. In his hand, he carried a large manila envelope and a smaller white business envelope. After him came Art and Brian, both wearing bright yellow slickers. Then an older man, his flannel shirt untucked in back, hanging out under a dirty canvas jacket. The last man's face was red and strangely raw; Kara thought he looked as if he'd been outside for a long time.

"Sorry to disturb you," Lyle said, "but we need to talk to Chuck. He asleep?" He took off his hat and held it in the same hand as the envelopes.

"No. He went out. I don't know where." She was looking at the floor, holding her arms tight against her body. Kara thought: Christ, Mother, could you look more guilty? Why don't you just *tell* them?

"Went out?" Pointer repeated it blandly. "It's late on a rough night, isn't it?"

"I don't know." Gretchen's head trembled slightly and her eyes began to shine with tears. "I was asleep."

"I . . . I saw him," Kara said. The hardest part in dealing with cops was that you were supposed to act nervous. She didn't stare at Pointer's eyes but looked directly at one, then the other. And she made every statement sound like a question: "He told me he was going for a walk? He has some insomnia, you know? And . . . and he has to walk it off, usually?"

"Did he say where he was going?"

"Just along the highway is all." She did not want them prowling the beach. She almost added something about it being too wet to be off the road but restrained herself. Don't oversell it, she thought.

Gretchen had relaxed enough to release her arms, but in the next moment she trapped them again, this time slipping her hands into the pockets of her robe. She said, "What exactly did you want from him in the middle of the night?"

"When did he go out?" Pointer stared at Kara. "You were awake when the insomnia was bothering him, obviously."

Gretchen snapped at him: "Exactly what is this about?"

Pointer kept his eyes on Kara for an instant, waiting for her to reveal something more, but she just looked back—at one eye, then the other. "We have a little money problem," he said. "And another matter."

Her mother was trembling, but Kara couldn't tell if it was obvious to them. "Shut the door," Gretchen said to her. Then, to Lyle: "What do you mean?"

Lyle opened the smaller envelope and pulled out three hundred-dollar bills. "First, there's the money. Seems Art was going through Leo's old albums. He pulled out a Tony Bennett record and this came with it."

"For this you woke us up at this hour?"

"We saw your lights on." Lyle made it sound like both an explanation and an accusation. "You don't find this at all unusual? That Leo—whose first words in his will were that the money is all gone—has three hundred dollars stuffed in a record album? I guess I find it a little unusual."

"Well, I'm not sure," she replied. "I didn't know Leo and I don't know what his mental condition was." Lyle just waited, nodding slowly. "Well, what am I supposed to say here? Obviously, if we had known the money was there, we might have talked it over with Art before he took the records. Maybe there's more money stuffed inside Perry Como."

"No. Appears not. That possibility was quickly and pretty clumsily explored by Bartok, about two minutes after Art found this."

"Bartok?" Kara said. "The guy from the bar?"

"He was there . . . at the bar . . . when I pulled the record out," Art explained. "After I got home, I decided I didn't want to drink alone after all, so I called Brian and we decided to go to the bar. I brought along the records just so we could check them out and . . . the money . . . I mean," he stammered, "it just flew out on the bar. Everybody got all lathered up about it. Bartok grabbed the other albums and dumped them out on the bar, the jerk. While he was storming around, we went to get Lyle. I thought they might be coming out here next."

"Out here?"

"They were highly excited," Brian said.

Lyle touched Brian on the arm. "Let's not get people all panicky. Bartok and the rest of those boys are pretty upset about losing their money to Leo. They were suspicious before and this only adds to their suspicion. It's late, though, and it's a lousy night. So I wouldn't expect to see them. But you can't be sure."

"Well, can you give us some protection?"

"I'd like to, but Mr. Blaylock"—here, he nodded to the raw-faced man in the canvas jacket—"and I have another matter on our hands. I'd feel better about leaving if Chuck was here."

Art said, "Brian and I'd be happy to hang around, Lyle. You and Blaylock go about your business and we'll stay here, at least until Chuck gets back."

"And you think he's just out walking off his insomnia on a night like this?" Lyle was baiting her now.

"I don't think the weather has a lot to do with it, Mr. Pointer."

Kara added, "He does it all the time back home. Even when it's twenty below, he'll go out walking."

"That's true," Art said. He looked directly at Kara and nodded. Kara couldn't tell if he was lying for Chuck or if, in his youth, Chuck had wandered the highway at night. "Old Leo always said he expected to find him run over some morning, he spent so much time walking the shoulder."

"OK." Lyle pulled a business card out of the inside pocket of his jacket and set it on the dining-room table. "I want to talk with him when he gets back. Have him call me at my office tonight, the moment he shows up." He sighed.

In that instant, the kitchen door slammed open, blown by a gust off the lake, and the crash of breaking glass filled the warm dining room. "Jesus," Pointer yelled.

Kara met her mother's eyes, and for that instant they

shared the same image: Chuck, dragging the drowned woman's body over his shoulder, had lost his grip on the door, or stumbled into it, shattering the pane. There would be no discussion, no explanation. That would be that.

Pointer was first in the kitchen. The others followed. Blaylock, moving stiffly, was the last to see Chuck standing barefoot in the broken glass, struggling to close the storm door, the water still running in thin streams off his hair and the muddy windbreaker. The wind howled and banged the door against the side of the house, over and over. Each time, more shark's teeth of glass flew out of the wood frame.

Art said, "Just stay there," and stepped over the broken glass to latch the outer door.

Gretchen said, "Don't move," but Chuck picked his way three steps across the floor to the kitchen table, cursing passionately as he went. He stood there, shaking his head and arms. Kara grabbed the dish towel from its ring by the sink and he took it. He rubbed his face, grimacing, then rubbed his hair. Then he stripped off the soaked windbreaker. "Look at the party," he said cheerlessly. "What's up?"

Lyle looked him up and down. "Where've you been?"

"Walking around. Couldn't sleep. What's it to you?"

"With no shoes? No shirt?"

"Shoes get a little dirty walking on a muddy shoulder, Sheriff. You can check 'em there on the landing. And I didn't know you were enforcing a dress code these days."

Lyle smiled thinly. "That was humorous. Wasn't it."

Chuck smiled back. Then: "Kara, get me some shoes and a sweater or something, will you?"

Kara had felt the numbness edging up, and now, seeing Chuck so at ease, she let it flow through her. He could not be this calm with Mrs. Ford's body still bobbing around in the lake. But how could he be so calm if he had found her, and dragged the soaking corpse up onshore somewhere. It was beyond calculating, so she simply ignored it.

By the time she returned—moments later—with clothes and a heavier towel, he had poured himself a glass of red wine and was drinking it, not desperately but with relish. Her mother was sweeping the floor and Pointer was looking less sure of himself. The three hundreds were spread out before him on the table's Formica surface.

"Look," Chuck was saying, "I'd like to help. But I don't have any idea about where this money came from. It's pretty obvious I didn't know it was in the album, isn't it? Art's a friend and all, but I'd be tempted to put that in my wallet if I knew it was there." He paused for an instant, then added, "You mind if I change my pants?"

Lyle shook his head and scowled. "You been in the water, Chuck?"

Chuck stopped, his hands on the strings of his sweatpants. "Is that supposed to be funny?"

Lyle shook his head again. "You want us to leave?"

"Doesn't bother me." Chuck dropped his pants to the floor and kicked them aside. He took the jeans from the pile she'd brought and slipped into them, squatting slightly to stretch the freshly washed fabric, sucking in his gut to let the zipper reach the top, the button slide home. "So explain to me again what you think I can do for you."

Before Lyle could answer, a vehicle pulled up in front, close to the house, so that a single headlight flooded the living room. A truck or Jeep, Kara thought. Too high for a car. Outside, the sound of that vehicle was joined with another, and another. Another headlight glared through the window at the base of the stairs; a moment later the small window high in the front door glowed.

"It might be more a question of what I can do for you," Lyle said drily. "Lock that back door, and don't show your face at the front. Art, please keep everyone here company." He set the manila envelope on the kitchen table, and walked slowly through the dining room toward the front door.

"What the hell is going on?" Chuck demanded.

"Relax," Art said. "Lyle can handle these guys."

Brian stepped close to Kara and patted her shoulder. "It's going to be OK," he said. "I can tell."

The sheriff put his hat carefully on his head, opened the front door wide, and filled the frame with his bulk. He stood there for a moment, then pushed open the storm door and walked out.

The wind and the door kept Kara from hearing what was said, but she couldn't mistake the urgency of the words, or the fury. The men outside were arguing intensely. Probably drunkenly. And she wasn't surprised when one of them burst through the door, the sheriff's arm around him at first, then dragged away as others pushed into the main room.

She didn't know the leathery old man who pushed through first, but following him were Bartok, his red beard wet with rain, and Gromek. Others followed. "All right, where is he?" Gromek croaked.

"Right here." Chuck stood at the doorway into the kitchen. "You want to talk to me, Gromek? Fine. You want to tear the house apart? Fine. I've got nothing to hide. There's nothing here. The money is gone."

"So how come three hundred dollars suddenly appears in a record album?"

"Pennies from heaven? How do I know? Are you suggesting I knew about it and just decided it was Art's— fair and square—because he got the records? You are dumber than you look."

Bartok grinned malevolently and moved forward.

"Stop." It was Lyle, who had stepped back inside the front door.

Bartok turned.

"I'm going to make this simple," Lyle said. "I told you boys to stay out and you pushed on by me. That's grounds for arrest, and I'm willing to do that." He walked slowly through the group until he stood face to face with Bartok. "I can call over to Bayfield and Washburn and get some help and arrest everyone tonight. Or I can arrest you gradually, one at a time, sometime when you're off by yourselves."

"You are a deputy of the people," Gromek said. "Your authority comes from us. And we are pissed off." Kara noticed that Blaylock, the red-faced man who'd come in with Lyle, had slipped from behind her and sidled next to Bartok.

Lyle didn't raise his voice. "And so what do you think you are going to do about it? I'm warning you boys— don't piss me off or I will call in the National Guard."

"We're going to go through this house—top to bottom," Gromek insisted. "I'm not necessarily saying Leo stole from us. But he wasn't himself at the end. Something snapped, and unfortunately it snapped while he was holding our money. Now we're going to look through every drawer and under every mattress in this place until we find what is ours. And if we don't find it, we're going to go through the shed and the flower beds and look under every goddamn bush for a mile around. Until we do find it."

"Who was the son of a bitch that first pushed past me?" Lyle demanded. "Was that you, Bone? Did you shove me out of the way? 'Cause if it was you, I might remember that."

"It wasn't me, no," said the leathery old man. He pulled off his black stocking cap. "I was after."

"I'm trying to remember who pushed me." Lyle turned back to Gromek. "Now listen. First of all, just because an old man misplaces three hundred dollars, it doesn't mean he has more just lying around where you could find it."

"You heard the will," Gromek protested. "That money is around. He as much as said so."

"I didn't hear anything like that."

"You're a fucking idiot, then."

Brian whispered in Kara's ear, "So we're all fucking idiots. So the term has no meaning."

"Second," Lyle went on, "you know how easy it is to hide ten thousand dollars or even twenty thousand? In hundreds? It's so small it's practically invisible. You actually think you're capable of finding it tonight, at two A.M., after you've been drinking? And how do you know that if one of you does find it, he won't just slip that little wad into his sock and forget to mention it to the rest of you. A person can make some pretty rash moral judgments in the early morning. Which is why I'm willing to forget that someone pushed me aside out there a few minutes ago. Assuming you all clear out of here right now."

Bartok didn't move. "We want this freak . . . this loser . . . to give us our money."

"I will seek a search warrant for this property first thing tomorrow," Lyle replied. "But right now, I want everyone out of here . . . and I mean it. I will discuss this issue with Chuck for about five minutes. After that time, I'm going to drive from one end of this island to the other looking for anyone behind the wheel of a car. And then I'm going to give them a breath test. And if I think they are above the legal limit, I'm going to lock them up. And I expect to be going over to Bayfield on this business in the morning—which means I'm leaving in a few hours, damn it—so I might not get around to unlocking anyone for a while."

"Who's going to watch them?" Bartok demanded, pointing at Chuck and Gretchen. "How do we know they won't try to skip out with the money?"

"Skip out?" Lyle shook his head. "Use your skull, Bartok. The only way off this rock is by boat, and Chuck isn't likely to go on anything smaller than the ferry. Am I right?"

Chuck didn't answer.

"He's not going anywhere without your knowing about it." He took a deep breath, shrugged, extended his arm. "Now, gentlemen . . . this is the door." Old Bone Torkson set his cap back on his head and jammed it down with two hands, so that it covered his ears. He stepped quietly out the door, and the other men filed after. As the last few passed him, Lyle made a special effort to look them in the face, nodding at each one. Blaylock shuffled back a few steps until he stood next to Art. Gromek—the last to leave—glared back.

Lyle shut the door but didn't lock it. Didn't bother to check on the trucks and Jeeps pulling onto the highway. He turned to Chuck. "Before I go, there's something else," Lyle said. "We may have a missing person on our hands."

Gretchen froze. "Who's missing?"

"We wondered if you had seen her," said Lyle.

They can't know this quickly, Kara thought.

"Who?" Gretchen's voice creaked. For an instant, Kara thought her mother would faint. Chuck waited, silent.

"Well . . ." Lyle didn't speak for a moment. Kara couldn't tell if he felt awkward or if this was a stupid cop mind-fuck. "Jeanine Blaylock." Kara recalled the aging Kewpie doll blonde with the short curly hair and red lips.

"I talked with her at the bar this afternoon," Chuck said. "She was at the reading too, but I don't think I said two words to her there."

"He talked to her," Blaylock said. Kara noticed his flannel shirt was ripped at the pocket. He stood stiffly, his elbows seemingly pinned to his side. When he spoke, his lips barely moved. "Outside the bar. People saw them."

Lyle didn't look back. "This is Stuart Blaylock. Jeanine's husband."

Disappearance solved, Kara thought. Who wouldn't bail out on a guy like that?

Chuck spoke to Lyle, not to Blaylock. "Like I said, she came out of the bar and we talked for a few minutes."

"People said they did." Blaylock squinted at her mother. "People saw them." Kara thought he was near tears. "I don't care where she went, I just want her back."

"Look, Stuart." Lyle took a half-step toward him but kept his eye on Gretchen. "Maybe you should go back out to the truck. This is police work. You're too close to it to be in here now."

"I just want to know she's safe," Blaylock mumbled. "That's all."

"She's not here," Lyle said.

"Show 'em the note," Blaylock insisted.

"Art, you want to take Stuart back to the car for me?"

Art took the distraught man by the arm, but Blaylock shook it off. "I'm staying here. It's my wife you're talking about." Art tried to take his arm again and Blaylock pulled away again, with more force. "Touch me again and I'll fucking kill you, Art."

"Whoa." Art chuckled. "You stay right where you are, Stuart. And I'll move far, far away." He backed off, wandered over to the wood stove, and sat down in the throne with the lion's-claw feet. "I'll be over here, Lyle," he yelled.

Brian yelled after him, *"Don't sit in Leo's chair,"* and Art stood up abruptly. Kara noticed that he was leaving small smears of black mud on the wood floor.

The sheriff rubbed his eyes and ignored him. "She got off work a little after four, stopped at home for a few minutes, and then went to the reading. She was expected back around seven-thirty, to have dinner with her mother and some relatives. It was a birthday party for a cousin. It isn't her nature to miss a family function. She never showed, and no one has seen her since. Then Stuart found this in his wastebasket."

Lyle opened the manila envelope and handed Chuck a small scrap of wrinkled pink paper. It had been torn from a cheap notepad and a ragged thread of red binding rubber still clung to the top edge.

Over his shoulder, Kara read:

Chuck, what I didn't say before (at the bar) was how emotional it is to see you. I expected you here for the funeral and when you didn't show, I figured you'd never come. Then to see your face, after all these years. It's like you've grown into your looks . . . if that makes sense. I'm so happy for you and your wife and to have a strong young daughter like that. You must be really proud. I don't mean to get anyone in trouble, but would it be too hard to see me for just a second while you're here? I really need to talk to someone. Can you get away to the old cabin we used to use? You were always the best.

The last two sentences had double pencil lines scratched through them.

Chuck shook his head. "She never . . . I don't know anything about this. She threw the note away. Obviously, she reconsidered."

"Maybe she spent the evening at this cabin she's writing about?" Pointer went on. "Where's that at?"

"Damn if I know. Art, you tell him. How many empty summer cabins did we break into when we were kids? Every winter there'd be one or two that we'd have as headquarters. We'd use the fireplaces for heat and just hang around. Then the next year we'd go somewhere else. Isn't that right?"

Art nodded. "It was nothing serious, Lyle. We'd just be kids horsing around." Kara could tell by looking at him that it was more than that, and Lyle probably knew as much, but that wasn't the issue at hand.

Pointer was openly skeptical. "She writes like she had a particular cabin in mind, doesn't she?"

"I don't know. Maybe she did." Chuck pulled on one

dry sock, then paused. "Maybe her memories of a particular summer are stronger than mine. She stayed around. I left. That changes you. There's a lot about this place I've forgotten. And if she wanted to talk with me, why the hell didn't she call? I've got a phone. She's got a phone."

Blaylock shifted his feet and muttered, "You know damn well she didn't want to talk, you little bastard."

Chuck stared at him coolly. "I don't know what she wanted, Blaylock. I haven't seen her in almost twenty-five years. You live with her. You know her needs better than I do."

That was rotten, Kara thought. She expected the older man to come at Chuck but he wasn't the type. Instead, his mouth began to twitch and then his jaw and he sobbed. "I don't care about all that, damn it. I just want her back." Brian looked nervously at Pointer and then the two men looked down. Blaylock went on: "It's going to freeze tonight and all I can think about is that maybe she's out there somewhere lost or hurt and if we can't find her now she won't make it through the night."

All the adults were unnerved now. By the tears, or maybe by the image of Jeanine injured and alone in the night. A fall on the rocky shore . . . a broken leg in the woods . . . Kara thought of the traps under the basement stairs, which had been designed to snap down on and hold the bloodied legs of wandering animals.

She was not moved by his crying, though. She stared at the man's eyes and saw an emptiness that made her worry. He does not love her like he says, she thought, or else it's a love I don't understand.

"I'm not going to find her here," Blaylock said. "Let's go."

Pointer turned wordlessly. Art nodded to Brian and they followed.

"Lyle," Chuck called after them. The cop turned and let the other men pass outside. "Listen," Chuck said. "No judge is going to give you a search warrant. There's no crime."

"That's what I was thinking. But it defused the situation, which was my top priority. We'll see how everyone feels tomorrow when they've sobered up."

"I don't know how long I'm staying, OK? I don't think I want to hang around too long."

Pointer didn't look at him. "Let me know when you're leaving."

"Fair enough. And you knew Jeanine was having affairs? Art told me earlier. I didn't want to say anything while Blaylock was here."

Lyle nodded. "There are signs that she was seeing someone. I expect to be looking into that."

"It would be important to know if he's got an alibi, wouldn't it?"

Pointer gave him a dismissive look. "I'll worry about the investigation here."

"Do you even know if this person lives on the island?" Chuck pressed. "Maybe she's over in Bayfield or Washburn?"

Lyle glared at him. "I doubt that Jeanine or anyone else was on the lake tonight, the way it's been blowing. I don't know what condition Jeanine is in, but she's somewhere on this island. And whatever's happened to her happened here."

"You sound pretty sure something happened."

Lyle said nothing for a moment. He worked the brim of his hat through his hands, contemplating. Kara thought it was another hammy attempt to draw out information, until Lyle blurted, "Something's going on. People are barging into people's houses in the middle of the night and money's falling out of the sky and now Jeanine's disappeared. Cripes, it's like fucking Halloween around here. They don't pay me enough for this."

# Lyle Pointer

*What did Gromek say? You derive your authority from the people? You earn your authority from the people? Your authority depends on the people?*

*Bunch of gimcrack philosophers lecturing me about my authority at three o'clock in the morning. Like life isn't painful enough already. Like there isn't enough hokum bullshit associated with law enforcement anywhere in the world, and then I have to land on an island full of cranks who haven't done enough of their homework to tell the Nonpartisan League from the National League.*

*Leo was a little different. He read a book every few months, from what I could tell, and he did know squat—if only that—about history. But the rest of them are inexcusable. Noses out of joint, and about what?*

*If they were farmers, I could understand. A few years back, when the farm economy was crumbling—what did Dad say?—almost half the farm sales in North Dakota were because of foreclosures. Men lost land that had* been in their families for a century. That's a world of hurt. Feeling completely impotent, you'd naturally see power in a new light. Of course you'd start your own politics. Of course you'd start your own religion. If you started blaming the Moonies and worshipping the sun, it would not surprise me in the least. The fact that some of those farmers blamed Jews and worshipped a vengeful Christ showed a lack of originality, but it was right in line with my conception of human nature.

But these clowns? I don't know what their beef is. They've got their boats and trucks and there's not a one of them that can't find the time to go deer and pheasant hunting every fall and fishing every weekend from May to September. They've got satellite dishes and beer money.

People in India, they don't even know how to dream about this kind of splendor. They lie down in bed at night and the most they can dream about is a little more rice, a few hours out of the rain, a solid shit. If they found them-selves living like these clowns, they'd be instant red-necks. They'd bitch about their taxes but they'd pay them. Grinning. They would be so stunned by their good fortune that they couldn't think beyond what a wonderful system we have, that gives people such wealth and free-dom. They'd turn in their Hindu cards and become God-fearing, churchgoing, family-loving rednecked Christians for the NRA. You take a guy from Bombay, give him a hunting rifle and a satellite dish and a trailer in northern Wisconsin, and you've made yourself a purebred ex-Hindu redneck with three mean dogs in the front yard.

Gromek and Bartok and the rest of them—including Leo—I don't know what they think they are. Posse Comi-tatus? Make me laugh. The real Posse boys thought Viet-nam was a conspiracy to lure good Christian white boys *into sex with Asian women, diluting the race. But these clowns, they were all over the kids that didn't want to go to Nam.*

*So what are they? Government-hating fascists? Half-baked libertarian anarchists? Truth is, I can't bring myself to talk politics with them unless I'm full of beer, and then I'm too nervous. They have an ambivalent sense of law and order. My authority comes from them, as they like to say, and they're always about two cc's of liquor or testosterone away from trying to take it back. A couple of Posse assholes killed three marshals in North Dakota back in the eighties, and that never leaves my mind.*

*We caught those guys. It took men and money and years of hunting but the law is persistent. Not absolutely persistent. Not by any means. But it's a hell of a lot more determined than the leaf-in-the-wind, you-go-your-way-I'll-go-mine, every-man-his-own-king bullshit these loopy bastards subscribe to.*

*Here's the difference: If it was up to these boneheads on a cold, stormy night, they'd crawl under a quilt and praise Allah that they don't have to leave the house. They wouldn't go over to Bayfield to see about a missing woman and getting a search warrant signed or anything else. But I would. I'm just that stupid.*

# Fifteen

## 3:00 A.M.

Gretchen waited for the taillights of the truck to disappear and by then it didn't matter anymore. She didn't have to break down and thought she might not even be able to. She just looked at her daughter and wondered how horribly scarred she would be and for how long.

Forever, she thought. These are the things that you never get past. Some night twenty years from now she'll be in bed with her husband, with her children asleep down the hall, and she'll wake up screaming and she won't be able to tell them why.

Together they had conspired to hide the remains of a human being from the police. Because they were afraid they would get in trouble. Now they could never go to the police. No matter what happened. They would put her in jail and her daughter in a county home if they found out.

It was Chuck's fault. He'd provoked those people

years ago and now, when an accident happens, when it looks bad, he has to do this. It was disgusting. It was not the way she wanted to live or to have her daughter live.

It was not right.

It was not good enough.

He was honest and funny and he looked good in jeans. He was enough of what she needed, but he was too dangerous. Before, she had not seen it in him. But here it was. Now, even if they got off the island she would see it in him. She was absolutely sure he had not killed the old woman, but he had done something almost as bad. He had twisted her daughter's head and made her look directly at something hideous and disgusting and put her at risk and that was not right. She had been violated and it was his fault. Maybe not entirely his fault, but she didn't care. It still wasn't good enough.

Damn him.

But then she put her arms around Kara and the heavy sweet scent of her daughter's hair comforted her. Kara returned the embrace and she was neither panicky nor delicate. This girl is strong, Gretchen thought. Then Chuck put his arm around them both and at first it seemed an intrusion but she didn't flinch. She did want him there. He spoke softly and firmly and she felt protected.

Maybe he was exactly right, she thought. This was life, after all. People threw chaos and destruction and decay at you and you fought it back any way you knew how. As long as you kept beating it back, you were winning.

This hadn't run its course yet and, in fact, would never be truly finished so long as they held the secret among themselves, but he was beating it back expertly. Winning for now.

She tried to tell him about the diary but he hushed her.

"It doesn't matter right now," he said. "Right now we need to take care of each other."

She looked first at Kara, then up at him. Her joints ached terribly and she was exhausted, and when she looked up his eyes were open and honest. So she believed him, because she was too weak to do otherwise.

There is a sign in that, she thought. If he were really dangerous, the adrenaline would kick in. Your gut would pulse with it; your legs would flex and twitch and plead with you to run. If he were really bad, you could not be so bone-weary in his arms.

And, of course, as she thought it, she recognized that she was absolutely wrong. When you are truly bone-weary, you fall where you stand.

He let go the embrace and motioned for them both to sit on the couch. This little conversation was going to focus on Kara, because she was the weaker link. Gretchen would crumble at some point—who would not?—but she had not reached her limit. Kara he did not know well enough. She was a teenager—sullen, erratic, constantly swinging between fear and overconfidence.

He went over it all, slowly. They were a family. Bad start: She would not know what that meant. She had grown up in a neighborhood where half the families had single mothers. The idea of constant support, of people hanging together through the bad times—it was a joke to them. Cynical little bastards. So he tried to explain that this was what families were about. Like he knew.

She listened, but he wasn't sure she bought it.

OK. He tried again. Less soap this time, more cold water: They had committed a crime. It was not their fault, but circumstances had forced it on them.

That part she got. She knew about being blameless and still having the cops on your tail. Teenagers were a colonized race, bound by culture and common persecution.

He paced the floor, repeating that he had done nothing to be ashamed of, nothing unethical, nothing truly wrong. He was innocent. But the people on this island were bloodstained. They all killed animals for sport. Even the women. The men had all killed in war. They—his father's friends, anyway—had sworn to kill the government agents who wanted their tax money, who wanted their submission to authority. Even the best of them spent their winters brawling because there was nothing better to do. Violence was in their bones, and when they looked at him, they assumed the same. When there was an accident, they assumed violence.

They'd assume he was a killer because they were. He and Gretchen and Kara could not give them a chance to be proved right. *They must all stick together.*

Gretchen asked about Mrs. Ford's body, so he told them what had happened—leaving out the worst, the lying in the ditch with her dead mouth pressed against him—as he built a fire in the iron stove.

He broke up the kindling and lit it, describing how he'd had to wade in for her. When he got to the part where the water reached his thighs, where he could feel the horrible buoyancy of it, and still she drifted away, he turned to them. He wanted to see from their faces if they understood, and knew that of course they did not. Could not. He started to relate it in minute detail, because he wanted to convey to them how wretched the water felt lapping at his crotch, how disgusting the smell of the lake, and how treacherous the footing. But then he stopped, afraid that he was sounding obsessed, weird, fixated. He didn't want them to doubt him, not now. So he turned back to the stove, huffed on the small flame he'd midwifed in its blackened guts.

He explained that he had left her in the shack and would have to go bury her now. It was a conscious decision to describe that little building as a shack and not as a cabin. He didn't want them wondering about Jeanine.

Then he realized the foolishness of telling them exactly where Mrs. Ford was, where she would be buried. Anything could happen. Ten years from now, Gretchen might meet someone smarter, richer, less troublesome, and demand a divorce. You never tell a potential ex-wife where the bodies are buried. Or Kara might be born-again and crave the release of confession. She might just decide she hated him and want to get even.

"I'm telling you both everything," he lied. "I want you to know exactly what we're into here."

He gently fed in the last split logs from the big basket on the braided rug. He brushed his hands, stood, and went to find a shovel and dry boots and a heavy coat. It would freeze tonight.

Kara watched him go and for the first time was truly frightened for herself and her mother. He had changed over the past twenty-four hours. Now—when the pressure was on—he was giving her the earnest eyes. The honey voice. The "we're all in this together, kid," the "you and me against the world."

He was acting like a pimp. And when he started telling them where she was and how she would be buried, her only thought was that the more they knew, the more guilty they became. This isn't honesty, she thought, this is blackmail.

That didn't mean that he'd killed the old woman. What would he have done that for, anyway? The diary? He hadn't even looked at it. It had been an accident and the people here—the people who expected and maybe wanted him to be evil and crazy—they had made it hard for him to be up-front. Fair enough. But this wasn't over yet, and if you're in the middle of a crisis you want your people to be up-front with you.

Instead he gave her the trembling lip and wet eye. The cheap family rap. The poor nonviolent me. The threat of jail.

My butt, she thought.

He got dressed and went down to the basement. Her mother shut the door behind him, then came over and sat by her in front of the wood stove. She put her arm around Kara and pulled her close. "The worst of this is behind us. But that doesn't mean it's over. You and I and Chuck are going to spend a great many years of our lives sorting through this. I know that. But right now I just want to get through it. Period. You think we can hang on?"

"We're doing OK so far, I guess."

"Well, no, we're not. I feel like we're letting Chuck lead us around. He's making all the decisions and I don't like it. When your father left, I swore I'd never do that again . . . but here I am." She pulled a loose strand of hair behind her ear. "He said they'd never believe it was an accident. He knows. At least he knows better than we do." She pulled the same loose strand back. "But I don't like it. I don't like it. Not telling Lyle is the most danger-ous, destructive thing I've ever done. So I should have decided—personally—to do it. I shouldn't have deferred to anyone."

Kara stared at her mother, thinking: You've become an

accomplice to a serious crime that could lead to murder charges. You've dragged me into it too. But you don't talk about whether it's right or wrong. For you, it's a control issue.

He had put on a thick sweater, an old one of Leo's. He was worried about the cold. He had to get her into the ground before it froze. He worried, too, that the rain might turn to snow and make it that much easier to track his movements, find the bare spot in the underbrush where she was buried.

He figured someone might be waiting for him, slumped in a parked truck on the shoulder of the road, a hundred yards down. Or squatting in a poncho, under an evergreen, out of the rain.

They'd stand outside in worse than this to kill a deer, he thought. They'd definitely do it to get me.

He'd pulled on an old blue parka and gloves and rubber boots and clomped down the stairs to the basement. Gretchen closed the door behind him. He knew he could not turn on the lights. If he did, and they were watching from the beach, he would be playing into their hands. So he used his touch and memory to negotiate the stairs and the landing at the bottom. The sky was still overcast, but it yielded enough light to let him shuffle to the windows that faced the beach. He stood there, studying the trees and rocks, trying to pick out a human form waiting for him. Nothing moved; no cupped matches flared; no cigarettes glowed.

He clicked on the flashlight for an instant, spotted the shovel against the wall not three feet away, and grasped it without moving. He put his hand on the dead bolt and found—his heart thumping once, twice—that the door was already unlocked. How long had it been unlocked? Probably since before supper, when Kara was cleaning down there.

He froze. Listened. Heard only the wind knocking the door against its frame. He comforted himself by thinking that if anyone had come in and hidden in the basement, he would have heard their breathing, their rustling, by now.

He slid outside, the cold blasting him. This time he went east along the back of the beach, scuttling over the rocks and branches. When the beach ended one gentle curve and began another, he ran past the point and quickly hid himself in a thicket of scrub trees. If people were following him, they would have to run now to catch up. They would make themselves visible. He waited, listening for voices or footfalls over the crash of the waves. No one appeared, so after a few moments he continued his low scramble. Another hundred yards and he came to a run-down A-frame, its windows shuttered for the winter.

He jogged around the A-frame, slowed as he approached the highway, then stopped. No trucks on the shoulder or the cabin driveway. He moved quickly across the road, dropped into the ditch. No one yelled. No one followed.

More at ease now, he trotted along the shoulder to the path and slipped into the woods. He slogged through the mud for a few moments before it hit him. When he shined the flashlight back over the path, it confirmed his fear. With each step, he was forming a neat cast of his boots. This was even worse than snow, he realized. If it froze tonight, the trail of footprints would freeze with it. Four months from now, an investigator could brush aside the snow and find evidence of this late-night trek as clear as if it had been chiseled into the ground. A good cop could even guess at the time. ("On November 30, the rain was pretty heavy after midnight, and the ground froze up around three-thirty A.M. So I would say that whoever made these prints was walking along the path between those two times.") If it kept raining, the prints might be washed out. If it stopped, he was stamping out a trail that would lead them directly to the mound—also preserved by the cold—that was Mrs. Ford's grave.

"Rain, you bastard, rain," he said out loud. And he made a note to destroy the boots. Or maybe bury them with the old woman and walk home barefoot.

When he got to the shack, he stopped. Sucked in a big gulp of air. Reminded himself of what was within. He shined his flashlight on the handle and realized that the door was not completely closed.

He hesitated, thrust it open. Shined in the flashlight. Screamed.

A huge raccoon had found its way into the shack and was sniffing eagerly at Mrs. Ford's corpse. It wheeled around at Chuck, bared its teeth, hissed. Its tiny feet scratched at the dirt floor.

"Out! Out!" Chuck yelled. He stepped into the room, leaving the door open wide, and swung at the beast with the shovel. "Git. Git." The raccoon backed up, its tail brushing against Mrs. Ford's neck, and hissed again. Chuck backed off another step. The animal hissed once more, then abruptly ran out the door.

Chuck slammed it shut. "Damned animals," he said. He wondered if they were especially carnivorous now with winter approaching quickly, if they would smell her and dig out the corpse if it didn't freeze quickly.

It struck him then. He would bury her here. Inside the

shack. A simple operation, really. Except that anyone searching around Leo's property looking for the money might step in here, see the disturbed dirt, be visited with a hunch.

He would cover his tracks. The fireplace apron—made of flagstone pieced around his Indian mosaic—was maybe five feet long, two feet wide. He would pull it all up, bury her, and then tamp each stone back in place. No one would notice that they had been disturbed.

He worked methodically. First, he turned the table over, removed the flagstones, and placed them on the table's underside. Then he started on the mosaic, extracting each stone and placing it on the top of the wooden box, re-creating it there. As he pieced the picture, he recalled how he had come to do it—not for money or from an aesthetic impulse but out of spite, because Leo had told him he had neither the discipline nor the imagination to create a thing of beauty. He had worked with precise attention, just to prove him wrong, and had learned much in the process. He had always considered it the beginning of his life as a craftsman. Now it looked crude to him, a thing done too quickly and inattentively. Or perhaps the ground had shifted over the seasons and moved the small stones.

As soon as he had cleared away the last of the mosaic, he began digging, piling the dirt on top of the flagstones. He wanted no piles of fresh dirt on the floor. The floor would remain well trod, aged.

He worked fast, finishing in less than a half hour. The grave was shallow—not quite four feet deep—but adequate. He dragged her into it, stopping for an instant to cross her arms over her chest. He did not say a prayer, but he looked at her for a moment, held her cold hand, apologized for the rough treatment.

He stood, walked to the small shelf, and pulled a wooden match from the box. From his jeans, he pulled out the note Jeanine had passed him after the reading, a small square of pink paper, lettered with red. He didn't reread it, but he clutched it in his hand for a moment. "You stupid, sad creature," he said. He lit the match, held it to the note. As the flame grew, he let go of the paper. He meant for it to drop into the open grave, but the wind from the chimney caught the burning paper, swirled it up, and then sucked it back to the cold hearth. It shimmied there an instant, almost immaterial. Then the ashes raised up, fluttered forward, and disintegrated over Mrs. Ford's corpse.

Chuck shoveled on the dirt, stomping it down as he went. Then he relaid the flagstones. Then, finally, the mosaic. A pile of dirt remained on the overturned table, and this he gently scooped up in the shovel and carried outside, where he flung it into the woods. He turned over the table, brushed the dirt off the top, took a last glance around the interior. He clicked off the flashlight and went outside, into the still-falling rain.

# Sixteen

Kara drifted toward the wood stove, thought about adding another log to the blaze, then drifted off again, to the floor-to-ceiling bookshelves near the stove.

The books were mostly old and yellowed, the titles printed in block typefaces from the forties and fifties. Some were tattered paperback editions of Greek and Roman classics. Some were crusty leather-bound volumes by people she had never heard of: histories, studies of pioneers and Indian culture, theories of economics. A few pulse-pounders—*Rendezvous in Rio* and *My Enemy, the Crocodile* stuck out—and an atlas and all the oddments that accumulate after nearly three-quarters of a century of reading and never throwing a book away.

Not much here, she thought.

One paperback had lost most of its spine, so that she couldn't read the title. She pulled it down, read the title out loud: *"The Journals of Kierkegaard,"* and riffled the pages. A heavily underlined passage, dated August 25, 1836, made her stop.

"When Goethe had accomplished the transition involved by a return to classical antiquity," the entry read, "why did the age not follow him, why did it not follow Hegel, why does it have no effect? Because they both limited it to an aesthetic and speculative development, but the political development had also to go through its romantic movement and that is why all the romantics of the new school are—politicians."

"Vice versa," Leo had added in the margin.

"Duh," Kara said. She read the passage again, and once more, and still didn't understand it. Irritated, she scanned up the page to an earlier entry, where Kierkegaard had wondered: "Is it true that I should not laugh at my own jokes?"

She flipped another few pages, found another underlined passage: "I have just returned from a party of which I was the life and soul; wit poured from my lips, everyone laughed and admired me—but I went away—and the dash should be as long as the earth's orbit ——————————————————————————— and wanted to shoot myself."

Kara nodded to herself, then read Leo's note: "Fool."

Fool? she thought. OK, Reverend, let me peek into your thoughts. And see if it doesn't give me the heaves.

Carrying the Kierkegaard book, she dropped onto the couch and grabbed the old man's diary. She began to flip through it, expecting a passage here or there to project itself forward. But page after page was jammed with useless metaphysics and petty finances.

She stopped at random, read until she lost traction,

flipped ahead. Suddenly, a name caught her eye: "August 22, 1990. Mary's birthday."

She skimmed ahead, but Mary wasn't mentioned in the rest of the entry; it detailed the cost of repairing the church roof after an ice dam had pushed water under the shingles. But the mention of the name had pushed Mary into Kara's consciousness. She drifted off for a moment, wondering how Mary had been drawn to the man her mother later married. After what about her was attractive to this man who was later attracted to her mother.

They were younger then. She was fun. Chuck had said wild, but in her mind, Kara thought he meant that she was just fun—rowdy, funny, spontaneous. Wild, to Kara, meant drug vials and firearms. Maybe Mary was pretty. Maybe she was sexy. Maybe she was available. They didn't have many choices, with only a few dozen kids living on the island. Maybe it was cheap wine and pheromones. Maybe it was cheap wine and politics.

She'd asked him about the war several times. Once, using words she had heard older people use, she'd asked, "What was it like to be working for peace during a war?" and he told her that he had not done that. "I didn't fight, and I didn't fight the fighting. I just went on with my life."

"Details?"

"There are none. I finished high school. Hung around for a year. Moved down to the Cities. Took a few courses at the U. Dropped out. Same as kids have always done. If you weren't worried about the draft and you didn't follow the news, you didn't have to pay any attention to the war."

She had pressed him: "It didn't affect who you knew? Who you hung with?"

"Oh, that. Sure. You could only run with people who hated everything about this country." He paused, and she expected him to flash a smile, but he wasn't joking. "If I'd met your mother then, I would never have gone out with her. From what she's told me, she was a nice, straight girl. Absolutely no chip on her shoulder. No bitterness. No contempt. Peter Pan collars and circle pins. I was repelled by girls like that."

Now Kara was smiling. "So you could only date within the church?"

"If I had brought your mother to my apartment, or to a party, she would have been completely creeped out. She would have gone to the bathroom and climbed out a window. I'm not kidding. And my friends would have mocked me."

"She was a normal," Kara concluded.

He started to shrug but stopped, held his shoulders in a tight hunch. "Yeah, but it wasn't about looks, really." The shoulders relaxed. "Style was a marker for good and evil. Circle pins were the sign of the devil. You only knew women who looked like they were on the right side. It didn't really matter how corrupt they were."

Now she wondered: And that was Mary?

She picked up Leo's diary, began to flip again. Nothing for ten or fifteen pages, then the names began to leap out.

She skimmed the entry marked December 31, 1990, and muttered, "Jesus." She read it again, closely now:

Every year on this day I remember it. And every year I remember it differently.

This year I've determined that Art was a fool to let it rest, to complain so weakly. If they had searched me, they would have found the watch. That would have proved nothing, but it would have raised suspicions, maybe led them to test the water in her lungs. Then maybe they would have been precise and clever enough to find shampoo in the water. But he was a weak young man then. Weakened by the war. He'd pushed himself to kill but not to understand. That's what a soldier does.

Not just soldiers. No one asks the hard questions. Sensible, since no one answers them, either. Still you would think people would exact more information. About everything. These fools gave me their money—rent money, food money, retirement money— thousands of dollars—on the basis of a very brief song-and-dance. If I'd given it all to Fullerton with the same empty-skulled enthusiasm, there'd be nothing left today.

Of course, if I'd been really cagey, I might have been able to do even better than I did. Everything would have felt like those first few months, when we were all really rich. I got used to it. When the bank started to fall apart, I couldn't go back to being penniless. I couldn't give it back. I wanted it for myself.

And I wanted to leave something behind for him. It's a tragic admission . . . but money was the only thing I could think of.

Was it wrong? Sure. Is it more forgivable because I didn't intend to do it? Because I never had the courage to forthrightly cheat people? Or is it worse that it was an act of such repellent weakness?

Strange how this feels. I guess I expected that stealing a large amount of money would be thrilling. Like robbing a train, Jesse James–style, push the safe off the railcar onto the cinders, blow it while the women scream and turn away, money flying into the air. This wasn't like that. This was filching. Even if it was a pile of money, it didn't thrill me to take it. I didn't feel like Jesse James. I felt like a pussy.

So now I guess I'll give it to my son, who was a pussy but now seems like he's making his way to becoming a man. I also want to give him back that artifact of the end of her time. I told him I would, one day, when he straightened himself out. Before, he was too weak to trust. He's older now. Working. Steady. If he can stick with this woman and her child, if he can show a little backbone, then I'll see it returned to him. His freedom and the money, too.

Kara tucked Leo's diary gently under her arm and forced herself to walk to the bottom of the stairs. "Mom?" she said softly. She climbed one step, then another. Then she ran. "Mom?"

# Blaylock

*Papa said patience is a virtue and I've for sure made it mine. I can wait the little bastard out. A warm sleeping bag for cover and a good hat and a little Canadian and there's no man or animal I can't outlast. Truth is, I like waiting. I go, One-Mis-sis-sip-pi. Two-Mis-sis-sip-pi. Three-Mis-sis-sip-pi. I like the feeling of each little second squeezing through me. No distractions. Nothing to turn you away from the passing of your time. I forget stuff sometimes, but it doesn't matter when you go second by second. There's always something else coming. Live like this, you don't need to remember. Nothing.*

*Too many busy people. Don't even know they're dying, they are so full of themselves and their importance and their busyness.*

*You're alive when time starts to crawl.*

*You can concentrate on little shit. Sitting here with the window down, you notice what life is. You feel the cold burning in your lungs. Wanting a smoke so bad makes the feeling even stronger. The smell of an entire summer turning to rot and waste under the rain.*

*You can't miss it sitting here, window open. You can hear a tempo in the rain—not just the steady drilling of drops on the hood but waves of drops. And at the same time there is the rhythm of time:*

*One Mississippi.*

*Two Mississippi.*

*. . .*

*. . .*

*Damn. Can't do that. Too comfy and you're cooked.*

*Other times like this, say in a duck blind, I've drifted off and when you shake it off you're groggy. Not tonight. Same hat, same whiskey, same shotgun, but tonight I'm ready as soon as I come to. Primed.*

*Funny how this is like Korea. Time creeping along and at the same time you know you're going to have action soon, life-or-death action. That was Pusan. Other places I can't remember the names of now. Like Korea too in the cold and rain. But you were alive then. They could kill you but in the moment before that . . . in the weeks before that . . . you were alive. Weren't you? You were so jazzed up and then you got home and it felt dead. Some guys can't stand the feeling, but it was OK for me. I could handle it.*

*He'll show. He'll wait till his woman is asleep and then he'll make his move. I'll be behind him and when I kill him Jeanine will be changed. I can't explain how, but I know that this particular hell will pass if I can just kill him and she knows why I did it. Will I do time? Maybe. Maybe not. Leo's kid's a prick.*

*A warm sleeping bag and a little whiskey and I can outlast any animal, anybody. Pusan or the Dakotas or here. I like it.*

*I'd know if she was lost or hurt. She's OK. Sad but OK. She's waiting for him at some cabin. Not far from here. I can tell that. And more. I know things. When life goes by so slowly, you get a good look at it. Things are changing, slowly, surely, second by second.*

*One-Mis-sis-sip-pi.*
*Two-Mis-sis-sip-pi.*
*Three-Mis-sis-sip-pi.*
*The best is yet to come.*

# Seventeen

3:45 A.M.

She had made a cup of instant coffee. Now the steam curled out of the stained yellow mug in her hands, against her belly, her elbows resting on the arms of the wingback chair.

She was waiting for him. She had insisted that Kara go upstairs, but Kara had refused, had, in fact, planted herself in front of the wood stove and pulled out a cigarette. Gretchen informed her that her smoking would bring repercussions—and not cancer, she added, but something in the short term. Not now, though. She was not going to have her attention or strength weakened by arguing with her daughter. Not tonight. Let the child smoke.

She had scanned the first half of the diary earlier, and found it dull. But after Kara ran up the stairs, holding the faded book away from her, and thrust it at her, confused about what it meant—after that she read with the kind of

**172**

concentration that doesn't come from curiosity or even intellectual passion. She had read closely because what she found could affect her daughter's survival. And her own. She had looked over at Kara from time to time as she read, always expecting to find her asleep and was always surprised when her daughter looked back clear-eyed.

She read the section Kara had found, and then read before it and beyond it. When Gretchen set down the diary, she was not sure of everything. But she had discovered plenty. She made coffee for her and Kara. Now Kara drank and tended the fire. Gretchen waited in the wing-back chair.

Billy had been gone just two months. Not enough time for her to want another man. There was not much of anything in her—not desire, not fear of being alone. Not even hatred of the man who had deserted her and their daughter.

To be so numb was frightening. And liberating—she was able to do things that had seemed impossible and go places that had seemed out of bounds. Not giving a rip was a universal visa.

She let the junior high school wrestling coach take her crashing through a bog in his Jeep and said nothing about the environment, and then she got drunk with him. She did not sleep with him and didn't bother to explain why.

She went to a gay bar with a girlfriend, and ran into a boy she'd taught ten years earlier. It should have been uncomfortable for her, but instead they got drunk together and she was funny—in a mean way—about other kids in his class.

After another night of barhopping with another girl-friend, she went to a party. Chuck was the first guy she saw when she came in the door—a skinny man about her own middle age playing guitar and growling a snaky blues song. She didn't find him especially attractive but he looked more interesting than the wrestling coach.

He had a husky voice and was faithful to the song, but a thin smile crept across his face in the pauses between lines. He knew better than to try to pull off these lyrics about skulls and rattlesnakes. Then, for an instant, he squinted one eye at her and the smile slid down into a leer. Come with me, the lyric went. It was a dare and she was taking dares then. And this was where it had taken her.

God damn your eyes, Billy, she thought now. If you'd stuck it out, I'd have stuck it out. I wouldn't have taken the dare that took me here.


He came in from the freezing rain—his body bent and chilled, his curly hair matted to his head, the water dribbling down from it and off his scarlet nose and chin—but she didn't try to help him. She let him shed the sodden parka and take the dish towel from the rack and put it to his head. She watched him kick off his boots, grunting, and pad into the living room to warm himself by the wood stove.

During all this time she said nothing to him and he didn't ask her why. He didn't seem to notice that Kara was smoking a cigarette. He stared at the flame, shattered by the grate, and said nothing to her. Nothing.

She handed him the diary, which she'd opened to a passage where Leo had described in macabre detail his image of how Chuck had killed Mary. Gretchen had been struck by the intensity of the old man's vision. His intoxication with the smallest facts—the warmth of the bath water, how difficult it must have been for Chuck to hold her soapy body under. Chuck's fear and stealth as he dressed her, how he must have brushed her hair, put her into the car.

He read the diary without expression, from the middle of the left page to the end of the page that faced it—but he didn't turn the page to continue. He handed it back to her.

"That's disgusting."

She waited for him to go on, and when he didn't she snapped, "That's all you can say?"

"You want me to deny it?"

If the denial is honest, she wanted to say. Instead, she said, "What is this about?"

"It's about Leo's twisted mind. It's about ... that whole diary is about the real world seen through his particular little piece of stained glass." Kara had left a pack of cigarettes on the floor. He pulled one out, lit it, inhaled. "I'm debating how much I should say."

"You're what? There's nothing to debate here." She crossed her arms. "You are not going to hold out on us."

"It's not about holding out." He blew out a thin stream of smoke. When he spoke again, it was with a calculating calm—as if he were talking to himself. "I want your trust. I need your trust. But the more you know, the more trouble you're in. The more liable you are." He paused, inhaled again. "I don't like this."

Abruptly, he jammed the cigarette through the stove grate and into the fire. He spoke quickly: "OK. Mary died. I didn't kill her. I loved her. But she died and the circumstances were complicated. It was an accident. Like tonight." He looked up at her suddenly, and she could tell he regretted drawing the comparison between the two deaths.

"Anyway, I was scared. I panicked. I guess I panicked, but I probably would have done the same thing in any case." He looked sadly at her, then down at Kara. "Is that enough to tell you? I don't want to get you implicated in anything if I can avoid it."

"You couldn't go to the police then? Just like tonight?"

"Worse than tonight." He shook his head. "You won't believe this, but it was even worse then. People hated my guts and I was a kid. Just a kid. They would've . . . I don't know what they would've done."

"What did you do?" Gretchen asked.

He shook his head. "Think about this. Think about how involved you want to be in something that happened twenty years ago. Think about how much you want on your conscience."

Kara said, "That's a cop-out."

A smirk crossed his face, then withered. "Maybe. But do you want to do jail time for me? Or do you want to spend your last few years of high school with your mother in jail? They'll give out twenty-four months for nothing."

"What did you do?" Gretchen repeated.

"In front of Kara?"

She had no way of knowing what he would say, but she knew that there were going to be no secrets from her daughter. If anything was going to be said, Kara was going to hear it. He knew it too. The prick. But she would not be diverted.

"What did you do?"

"This isn't easy for me." He folded his hands in his

lap. "It's like this. We were wild kids. Even after we were married. She slept with a few people. So did I. Mary and Art. Me and Jeanine. Jeanine and Art. People you don't know. It was no big deal to me. It would be today, because I'm older and I have different values and because sex is dangerous today. OK. It wasn't then, or it didn't feel that way to us. It was fashionable then. An open marriage. At least that's the way I remember it. But it got to be more than just sleeping around. After a while she started doing things to hurt me with it.

"Like she slept with my father." He stopped for a second, caught his breath. "It was sick. It was sick to sleep with him, but mostly the cruelty of it seemed sick. She knew how it was between Leo and me. He had everything. He was the big shot. I was a freak. Whatever I had Leo had, only he had more. Or better. Mary was the only thing I had that he didn't. And then she gave that to him too. Just out of sheer cruelty. I don't know why anyone would do that."

Oh, Jesus, she thought. He's going to confess to something here. What do I do if he says he killed her . . . ?

"We were getting ready for a big New Year's Eve party in Bayfield," he went on. "I went into the bathroom and she was in the tub. I told her to hurry up and she didn't want to hear it. She couldn't stand anyone telling her anything. She flipped out, got mean, and suddenly dropped that on me. She told me about Leo. Just like that. No regrets, no shame. Just ha-ha I fucked your dad.

"I don't know how it happened." He looked up here, for the first time since he'd started talking. He shook his head, still confused by the course of events. "She climbed out of the tub and started yelling in my face. We wrestled around, slapped each other, but I don't think I

ever really hit her. After a few seconds I left. I didn't
have the heart to keep fighting. I felt sick to my stomach.

"I don't know what happened. She didn't fall into the
tub, I don't think. I think she climbed back in and sat
down in the water and then passed out. Maybe she hit her
head when we were fighting or she got dizzy and fainted
from when I shook her. I think she'd been drinking, so
maybe that had something to do with it. I don't know.

"Anyway, I went downstairs. I had a beer. I waited and
tried to think of what I should do. When she didn't come
down, I went up. She was lying in the tub. Underwater.
Drowned.

"Like I say, maybe I panicked. But I knew what would
happen. I knew what people would think. That Chuck,
he's a seriously screwed-up kid. Christ, he was so crazy
for a while they had to throw him in an institution—you
wouldn't believe the stories about what he did. Then he
marries a tramp. They're smoking pot and screwing
around and they have no morals and they fight all the
time. Finally, he kills her. Motive? Well, you've got psy-
chosis, jealousy, drug-induced hallucinations. How much
do you need?

"I knew I was innocent. And I knew that no one would
believe me. Even today, people here think I'm a murderer.
Even though the coroner and the cops agreed she drove
off the main road and hit thin ice and went through."

He paused here, leaned over to open the grate and slide
in another log. "I got lucky. I knew where there was a
patch of thin ice about a hundred yards off the highway. I
put her foot on the gas pedal, put the car in gear, and got
out of the way. It went real slow and I was afraid someone would see it. Then it went right over the spot where I
thought it would break through. It kept going . . . creep-

ing along. I was afraid it would stop. Then I was afraid it wouldn't stop, that it would go all the way to Stockton Island."

"Stop it," Kara said.

"And then boom—she was gone. She hit a weak patch another hundred yards out and it was like the lake opened up and swallowed her. One bite."

"Mom," Kara said, but Gretchen cut her off.

"I was lucky," Chuck said. "It took me an hour to walk back to where we were living but no one saw me. Someone saw the wheel tracks and the hole late that night, but it was the middle of the next day before they could get the body. By that time, I'd called around, asking if anyone had seen her. Not much of an alibi but no one seemed to care. The coroner was hungover from New Year's Eve. None of the cops wanted to spend a lot of time on an early death that everyone had been expecting for a long time."

He crouched in front of the wood stove, warming his hands. He looked at Kara for a moment. "Sorry. Almost finished. I made one mistake. She didn't take off her watch when she was in the tub. It broke while we were fighting. The crystal shattered and got in the works and jammed the hands at eight-thirty. But someone saw the car drive through La Pointe around eleven-thirty.

"How important was the difference? I don't know. She was involved in some kind of violence three hours before her car went through the ice. It was fishy. Leo saw it right away and smelled something funny. They asked him to pray over the body, which he did. No one was paying real close attention, so he slipped the watch off her. Someone said they thought they'd seen a watch, but no one could figure out what had happened. So they forgot about it.

"Leo told me what he'd done and demanded an explanation. I gave him the story—just like I've told you—and he crumbled. Fell on his knees and started blubbering. To me, to God, to my mother. Blamed himself. I don't know, maybe he should have.

"When most people feel guilty and humiliated, they seek atonement. Leo turned around and dumped it on me. Within five minutes, he was off his knees and railing. Did I see what my life had led to? Did I think I could kill someone and get off? Could I fool God? Was I willing to change my ways and be a man? When I told him to fuck off, he held up the watch. Said it was my incentive to clean up my act. He could have destroyed the watch, you know. Could have thrown it into the lake or buried it or smashed it into a thousand pieces. Instead, the bastard hid it. And he held it over my head, said I could earn it— earn my freedom—by straightening out my life.

"I didn't kill him, which is what I would have done if I'd been a real killer trying to cover my tracks. I just left. Told anyone who would listen that the tragedy was too great to stay on around here. Which it was."

The new log wasn't catching fire, so he opened the grate, reached in with his bare hand, and gingerly shoved it. It still didn't flare up, so he grabbed the black poker and shoved the new log again, and the charred one underneath it. A thick flame erupted between the two logs, licking the bark of the newer one.

"The watch is still around here. By now, I guess, it's been completely forgotten, but Leo couldn't even die without letting me know that he still had that power over me. You remember in the will, he said I got the house and the crystal and whatever. Look around. There's no fucking crystal in this house. That was about the watch."

Gretchen didn't know if she believed him. Weighing a crazy man's diary against a twenty-year-old lie, she found no solid footing. So it was easiest to do nothing. Believe her husband. Accept his story. Accept his reckoning that he could not be honest with these people, about Mary or about Mrs. Ford. Trust that he had disposed of Mrs. Ford in such a way that she would not be resurrected. The other way—to go to Pointer, tell what she knew, implicate herself and her daughter—was too hard, too frightening. It would be the end for her husband and she could not do that unless she was convinced that he was lying. Lying and murderous. It was too much responsibility.

"So?" he asked. "Are you with me?"

"At this point," Kara said, "what other choice do we have?"

"Look," he said, "I know this isn't easy for either of you. You've both had Billy—someone you trusted—betray you. If I were you, I'd have a hard time trusting another guy. Especially when the situation is so horrible. But trust me." He looked squarely at Gretchen, then at Kara. "I'm telling you the truth. I won't hurt you. And I won't leave."

Gretchen sighed. "Like Kara said, we have no choice."

"OK," he said. "I'd rather you just trusted me. But that's OK. I'll earn your trust."

He picked up the diary. "My next job is to go through this and find out where he hid the money."

"Page 255," Gretchen said. "If I read it right."

"Any mention of the watch?"

"I don't know. I wasn't reading for that."

In the kitchen, the telephone jangled. Kara stood up to get it, but he stopped her. "I want you as far away from all this as possible," he said. He rose, looking at Gretchen. "You too. I'll get it."

He reached it on the fourth ring. She tried to listen, but Kara said, "Is this the right thing?"

"I think so, honey."

"I'm so tired, I don't know what to think. I need to sleep about sixteen hours."

"Soon. We'll get out of here tomorrow, I think."

Chuck walked quickly back into the room, reaching for the diary.

Gretchen asked, "Who was it?"

"Brian." Chuck's voice was clipped, his complexion even paler than before. "He thought I might want to know that Lyle is actually going to get a search warrant. He told everyone to stay away from here until he gets it. That way no evidence gets compromised. Then they can go over this place top to bottom tomorrow."

"I thought he couldn't get a search warrant without some evidence of a crime."

"He's going to be looking for evidence in connection with the disappearance of Jeanine Blaylock. That's the pretext, anyway."

"She's only been missing a few hours."

"Long enough around here, evidently." He began to flip to the back pages of the diary. "It's going to be awkward if they get here and we've knocked out any plaster."

"No problem," she said. "It's not in the house. It sounds like it's in some cabin near here."

"No," he said. She leaned over his shoulder, reading Leo's scrawl again:

How can that cabin be a place of shelter, a holy retreat, and a gateway to madness? How can it be my sanctum sanctorum and a safety-deposit box of my every perverse action? It is the nexus of all that keeps me from grace, and now it also holds my perfidious reward. Buried properly, before the fire, beneath the stony Indian, six feet down.

"Oh, shit," he cried.

"What is it?"

"Oh shit oh shit oh shit." He shut the book. "It's under her. Under Mrs. Ford."

"It can't mean that."

"She's at four feet. The money's at six. I have to dig her out."

"You can't. I won't have that. Just . . . just leave it there. You can come back in a few years and get it. Or just walk away from it. We'll get our house another way."

"I'm not walking away from that money. And I'm not going to dig her up a few years from now. I couldn't take that. I've got to get it and move it somewhere now. Tonight." He stood up. "What time is it? How can it not be daylight yet?"

"It will be light in an hour or two," she said. "And the mob will be here soon after."

"It won't take that long."

# Leo

*April 4, 1983—There was something the matter with him from the beginning. I saw it and did what I could but his mother stopped me, undercut me. When she died I tried to make up for lost time, but he was already past the forming years. He'd reached the age of conscience, and he was lost to me.*

*I never surrendered. I worked with him harder than any father I knew. Harder than my own father, certainly. I wanted him to embrace life. I got him a motorcycle as soon as he was old enough to ride one. Before that, I tried to teach him things. Hunting. Fishing. Swimming. I really worked on the swimming. Day after day I was out there with him. If you can swim in Superior, you can swim anywhere. But he couldn't cut it.*

*His last year of high school, things got worse. I expected a little rebellion—it's good for a young man to pull away from his father. But Chuck wasn't drinking or fighting or chasing girls. I don't think he was into drugs.*

*Still, something changed in him. He got strange in the way he acted. He hurt people. He hurt his dog. There were fires. No one could prove it was him, but everyone knew it.*

*Some people said he acted strangely to stay out of the military. That is wrong. I do not say it because I am his father, because I cannot admit to my son's cowardice. I admit that freely. But what he did had nothing to do with avoiding his national service. He could have become a conscientious objector. He could have gone to college. He could have driven the few hours north of Duluth to the Canadian border. The people there would have welcomed him. He would have gotten laid for his cowardice.*

*He is not stupid. He knew all this. He would not have done what he did when he had those other options. I remember him standing outside the store one afternoon. A group of boys and men, carrying on, him on the edge, his eyes glassy and bright at the same time. He started to say something and everyone stopped to listen. Nothing sensible came out. He tried again and stopped. Then he lost control of his bladder and wet the front of his pants.*

*That's when you stop wondering. In that instant, you know your son is not just a coward faking sickness. The injunction against fouling oneself runs too deep in human chemistry. You can't fake that. And there was no need. A man who can go to Canada doesn't pee on himself.*

# **Eighteen**

**4:15 A.M.**

She wanted her daughter to go to sleep, but was glad when she insisted on staying beside her on the couch. Gretchen didn't want to be alone with Chuck out of the house. Didn't want to be alone with him in it, either.

There are twists of fate, she thought. And there are corkscrews.

She felt scared and too stupid to know what to do next. Helpless, and the helplessness made her furious. And the fury made her hesitant, because she knew she was capable of rash action when she was angry. She was so angry that it paralyzed her, made her helpless and even more angry.

"We are trapped," she said to her daughter.

Kara shook her head. "We're not trapped. We can cut and run if we need to. Do you have money?"

"On me? Now? Not much."

"I've got about forty dollars. It's a start."

"Oh, Kara honey. What good is forty dollars going to do us?"

"It's a night in a motel and breakfast the next day."

Gretchen shook her head slowly. "If I was a good mother, this is where I'd lie to you. I'd smile and tell you that everything is going to work out fine. But the honest truth is I'm not sure enough to go to Pointer and I'm not sure enough to keep my mouth shut."

She closed the magazine in her lap. "He'll be back in an hour. He'll have the money. The locals will show up in a few hours and they'll tear up the house and find nothing. Then they'll give it up. That will be the end of it."

"No, it won't," Kara countered. "This will never end."

"They'll realize that Mrs. Ford is missing. But no one will know what happened to her. She'll never be found. They will suspect Chuck because she got the house from Leo. But it doesn't matter. They'll never find her."

"I want them to find her," Kara said. "I hate the idea of that old woman being stuck in the ground like a dead house pet."

Gretchen shook her head. "You and I want this more. We want to be a family, and we want Leo's money."

"We're keeping it, then?"

"I think that's what's been decided. Don't you?" Gretchen stood up, one hand pulling on the other. She thought: This is about everything in my life. "I can't sit here like this."

"So what do you want to do? Bake something?"

"Jesus, Kara."

"I'm just trying to ease the tension a little."

"I don't want the tension eased." She yelled this without meaning to. She took a breath and went on, more quietly: "I want to be absolutely keyed up and ready to react in an instant."

"Then let's tear this place apart. Let's finish going through everything in the house—top to bottom—before the locals start knocking out walls."

"I don't have the energy."

"It needs to be done, Mom. You came up here to protect what's ours. Who knows what'll be left in a couple hours."

He put his hand on the cabin door and for an instant imagined the single room filled with raccoons, digging patiently toward Mrs. Ford's corpse. It sickened him but he threw the door open and shined the light in. Nothing.

He went quickly to work, pulling out the stones that made the Indian's face, setting them aside until he had duplicated the high cheeks and headdress on the box in the center of the room. He smiled to himself. When he'd removed the stones before, he'd noticed that they seemed slightly askew. Uneven and out of position. He'd attributed it to shifts in the soil—freezing and heating and proximity to the fireplace. Now he knew it was because Leo had uprooted and replaced them. Lousy workmanship, he thought.

Somehow, under the guise of leaving me a treasure, he managed to find a way to destroy the first good piece of work I ever did, he thought. The bastard was relentless.

He turned over the table again, and placed the flagstones on the underside. The stones seemed heavier than before. He was tiring.

The spade came next. He put it gently into the still-fresh earth and lifted out a small pile of dirt. He wanted to move quickly but couldn't face the prospect of thrust-

ing the shovel deeply into the soil and hitting the soft re-
sistance of her flesh. He worked with fevered delicacy,
like an anthropologist trying to expose a more ancient
burial site.

A thousand years from now, what would an anthropologist think about this? he wondered. Buried under an
Indian symbol. In front of the fire. Buttons from her
housedress. Perhaps there'd be tools available for recon-
structing the note from Jeanine. What interpretations
would result?

He'd been drifting. He glanced out the small window
and was relieved to see that it was still dark.

Got to get back before sunrise, he thought. Then he
stopped and whistled at himself, saying, "Vampire, or
what?"

There was a small office at the head of the stairs.
Gretchen had passed by it several times in the fifteen
hours since they'd arrived on the island. Once, as she was
running down to the car on the way to the will reading,
she'd stuck her head in the door. She'd noted the old,
smudged electric typewriter on a gray metal desk. The
book-burdened, unvarnished wooden shelves, warping
on anodized metal racks. The fake-leather typing chair.

Now it was time to explore and catalogue. They only
had a couple of hours, so they split up. Her daughter
would rummage through the linen closet and then the
spare bedroom.

Gretchen was to dig through the office. At first all she
found was paper—notes from Leo to Leo, letters to friends,
business correspondence dealing with the church and his
political activities. She thought it odd that no one had
sued Leo for losing the money, no one had subpoenaed

all these papers and had an attorney paw through them instead of her.

She noticed a small wooden box—maybe six inches square, a couple of inches high—resting on a bookshelf. She picked it up, opened it gingerly, and scowled to see only a small manila envelope inside. She tipped the envelope, and a small brass key slid into her palm.

"Hey, Kara?"

"Umm." Her daughter poked her head into the room. "Find something?"

"Not really. I just found this in this box. Any idea what kind of key it is? The envelope is kind of like what we have for our safety-deposit box."

"Beats me. Nothing else in here?"

"Not yet." She pointed to the room across the hall. "My purse is on the bed. Go stick this in there, OK?"

Kara disappeared. Gretchen pushed the chair aside, noticed a file cabinet hard beside the desk, and, next to the cabinet, a small steamer trunk—old, rusted, the leather straps rotted but not yet broken off. The file cabinet held more useless paper. She opened the trunk, revealing a cloud of yellowed tissue paper.

She pushed the top layer of tissue aside. Underneath were smaller clouds—individual puffs and wisps. She grasped one, felt the hard center, peeled away the paper. At the core she found another wooden box, similar to the one that had contained the key, except this one was inlaid with other woods to form a radiant sun. The pieces were clumsily cut; the maker had filled the gaps with wood putty. The box was empty. She turned it over and saw that he had burned his name into the flat bottom: Chuck Hausman 1964.

She set the box down on the desk and opened another

cloud of tissue. Another box, this one strangely mis-shapen but with an intricate inlay of wood and polished stone. Other wooden boxes and simple disks inlaid with pieces of ceramic. The silhouette of a young man, done in reddish woods. It could have been a teenage Art, with a swollen nose. And a head that was flat in back and ran directly into his neck.

There must have been thirty pieces, dated over four or five years. She could see no improvement over that time, which made the collection both laughable and consoling. A testament to dedication in the face of inadequacy.

This is a man who doesn't give up easily, she thought. It's important that Kara see this.

He dug her out and pulled her off to the side of the cabin, noting that he would have to sweep away the tracks after he reinterred her. He did not bother to clear the dirt from her face. In his haste and the flashlight's fading illumination, he had managed to avoid seeing her face at all.

Nothing personal, he thought, and he meant it. Now that she was dead, nothing done to her body could be personal. The person was out of there. After people died, you couldn't show disrespect by what you did to their bodies, any more than by what you did to their cars.

He repeated the last part out loud. "It's like their car."

He went back to the grave and now buried the spade with force, using his foot to shove it deeply into the dirt. He concentrated his search on the area under the mosaic, moving soil from the middle of the shallow grave to either end. He became too eager and too sloppy, so that the dirt began to fly off his shovel and onto the cabin floor. He had to slow down, dig with precision.

He expected to find the money at least six feet deep

because that was where Leo had said it was. At five feet, though, he hit the metal box. It was a cheap file box, its metal so thin that the thrust of the shovel had put a deep crease in it.

Chuck probed with the spade, quickly found its edge, and levered the box out of the soil. He pulled it up, quickly brushing off the front. He tested the lock, found that it was either secured or frozen from corrosion. He put the shovel blade against it and jammed down once, hard, shearing it off cleanly. The force popped the top back, opening the box.

He grabbed the flashlight and aimed its failing beam inside. The sight of so much money made him suck in his breath. His chest hurt. He couldn't count it all now, couldn't take the time to pull out even one of the many thin stacks, each one wrapped with a dirty rubber band.

"Christ, Leo," he said. "What did you do?"

He had no time to think about where the money had come from, or how much there was, or how it would change their lives. He flipped the lid shut and carried the box close to the door. Moving quickly, he shoveled a few spades of dirt back into the hole, leveling out the bottom. Then he dragged her back across the floor and rolled her into the cavity.

The next steps came in a rush. He wrestled the table to the grave and tipped the dirt in, a bit at a time, leveling and tamping it each time. It was even more sickening work this time. Before, he had been too afraid to pay much notice to what he was doing. Now, he was calculating, and it was about money, and every time he stamped on the earth to pack it, he imagined that he felt the rebound of her soft body.

It was too slow. He was losing strength and he had the

money; both facts weighted every action, slowed every step. Eventually, the ground was ready for the flagstones. He heaved them into place and, in the flashlight's last feeble rays, he did a shoddy reconstruction of the mosaic. This time, the head looked square.

Using a small pine bough, he brushed the floor lightly, trying to hide the tracks of her body and the table, the impression of the flagstones. Next, the money would have to be stashed near the road. He tucked the metal box under his arm, flicked off the flashlight, and stepped outside. The first pale filaments of dawn arched over the roof of the shack.

"Home free," he said.


Kara had expected more from a madman's linen closet. Weapons, pornography, skeletonized infants. What she found was linen and half-consumed toiletries. And the spare room was . . . spare. Simple metal frame bed (nothing under it), faded chenille spread. A pole lamp, with one bulb pointed at the bed and the other at a table with no chair. The air smelled stagnant.

"Rose-for-Emily City," she said. She shut the door and went quietly downstairs, hoping to cop another cigarette before her mother finished in the office. She was trembling with fatigue and the wrong kind of excitement, and would have added a finger of Canadian Club to the cigarette but didn't want the confrontation. She was intent on preserving her strength.

The living room was colder now. The fire had burned down to embers and there was nothing left in the basket. She rejected the idea of going outside to the stack by the old shed, telling herself that she would be comfortable enough with residual heat and the old comforter. Then she recalled the wood under the basement stairs, along with the spiderwebs and gruesome traps.

Her mother had bolted the door to the basement after Chuck slipped out. Kara slipped it free, swung the door open, and fumbled for the switch on the other side of the jamb.

The bulb cast a dim light down the old stairs. She reached the bottom, turned slowly, then stopped. Something had changed since she was down here before supper. Prickly droplets emerged from her armpits, her forehead, between her breasts.

She scanned the room. The two orange-and-green-flowered sheets still hung motionless from the clothes-line. The door was unlatched; Chuck had left it that way the last time he went out.

She took a step forward and then saw it, almost put her foot in it. A large can of roof cement had been knocked off the workbench. The top had popped off and the tarry, black contents had oozed out into a gooey puddle, wide as a manhole. Someone had walked through it, leaving a trail of footprints that ended at the beach-side door.

She cursed, scanned the room again, listened. There was something else. The sheets didn't sway, though. No boots scraped behind the workbench or the washing machine. Somewhere, perhaps in the big sink, a drop of water landed with a smack. The black footprints were going in the right direction—out. She wanted to latch the door but didn't know if Chuck needed to come back inside that way. She hesitated. Nothing moved. She was alone. She was fine.

Still shaky, she took the three steps to the room under the stairs and opened the door. She first grabbed a stout oak branch. And another. Then her fingers reached out and encircled the cool naked foot.

Kara reeled back. The sound of her choked cry bounced off the walls and made her think someone was behind her. She spun around, spun back. The fear sizzled through her, then rapidly turned to nausea. She gagged but still opened the door wider and turned her eyes to Jeanine's damp corpse. The body looked as if it had been submerged: the woman's blonde curls drooped over her limp, pink-painted cheeks. Drops of water clung to the lashes around her still-open eyes. A small puddle had formed under the dangling foot. But whoever had done this had done more. She had been propped up obscenely on the firewood, her soggy sweater lifted to expose one breast, her skirt hiked above her waist.

Kara made a noise in her throat.

She slammed the door. It bounced off the frame and started to swing open again. She blocked it with her foot. She shook so violently that she had to sit down—but as soon as she did, the fear returned and made her stand. Chuck had seen her, after all. He had seen her and drowned her and brought her back here.

Suddenly, above her, the outside door opened. She could hear him in the kitchen, kicking off his boots as he called out for her mother. She heard him shuffle through the living room, then climb the stairs to the second floor.

They will get him now, she thought. They will find her when they come in the morning. Even if he buries this one too, we know where he put Mrs. Ford. We know about Mary. We know the watch is here somewhere. He is not getting away this time.

She mounted the steps silently, hoping to keep him unaware that she had been in the basement. Back in the kitchen, she shut and bolted the basement door. She went to the cupboard and prepared a diversion: Pulling out a glass and the bottle of Canadian Club, she poured herself a drink. She lit a cigarette.

She thought: They are still upstairs. You cannot call her away from him without his wondering why. Bring the smoke and the drink up with you. Generate as much emotional white noise as you can. Jam his radar. Climb the stairs slowly, because you are tired, because you do not have a river of adrenaline roaring through you. Know that he will be beside your mother and you will have to look at him. In the face.

She started up to their bedroom and then, abruptly, he was at the top of the stairs, peering down at her, his shirt off, feet bare, hands balled at his sides. "What's going on?"

Look in his face. "Nothing."

"What are you doing with that? Is that whiskey?"

"I needed one, OK? It isn't the first drink of my life. Where's Mom?"

"What have you got all over your feet?"

She spun around, saw the trail of black stains following her up the stairs. "Oh, shit."

"Where did you get in that?"

Her heart heaved up in her chest. "I went down in the basement to double-check the beach door. Which you'd forgotten to chain, by the way."

"I had your mother lock the dead bolt at the top of the stairs. Take those shoes off now and leave them on that rug by the front door. Are you sure everything is locked up?"

She pulled the shoes off quickly. "Yes, yes. Where's Mom?"

"Right here." Her mother was behind him at the top of the stairs. "What's all this?"

"Everything has to be locked up," he said. "It's important."

"I know, I know."

Gretchen came three steps down the stairs. In a whisper, she said, "He found the money, Kara. All of it. It's hidden down the road, so when they come tomorrow they'll . . ." Her voice drifted off when she saw the glass. "God, Kara," she erupted. "What is this?"

"Don't say it." Kara raised her hand. "I don't know what got into me. You want it?"

"No. Get rid of it."

"I'll just dump it out, OK?" Kara pulled her lips down tight, as though she were about to cry, and softly begged, "Come with me?"

Gretchen closed her eyes and sighed.

Kara waited until her mother took the first step, then turned, and led her into the kitchen. They had jackets there. Shoes. A door to the car.

She set the glass on the counter and positioned herself to see the base of the stairs that he would have to come down. She inventoried the dish rack, located the big French knife.

When her mother entered the room, Kara took her sleeves in hand and spoke softly, urgently, tersely—a kind of telegraph language: "She is in the basement, Mom. Jeanine is dead. In the basement. Under the stairs. I saw her. He killed her, Mom. We have to get out of here. Now."

Her mother looked into her face—the eyes, the mouth, the jaw—and for an instant Kara feared she did not believe her. Then the reality flooded over her and with it the horror. "Oh, God. You're sure? I have to see her."

"No! We need to go. Now. We can't let him know that

we know or he'll kill us too. We need to find Lyle and tell him. We need to get away. Now!"

"How do you know it's him?" Her voice was begging Kara to be wrong.

"Mother. She was all wet. He went to see her when he said he couldn't sleep. He drowned her and tried to hide her here. He's crazy, Mom. He's as crazy as they say he is."

"I don't have the keys," her mother said flatly. "The keys are upstairs. I have to go get them."

"Wait." Kara slipped into an old pair of boots—Mrs. Ford's? she wondered—that were standing by the back door. "OK. I'm right behind you." She pulled the heavy-bladed kitchen knife from the dish rack. Her mother took a wooden step forward, then another. Kara followed, two steps back . . . through the dining room, up the stairs. She waited in the hallway while her mother went into the bedroom.

She could hear Chuck. "What's going on with her. We can't afford to have her freaking out now."

"She's fine." Her mother sobbed. "I just need my purse there."

"Gretchen, what's the matter?" The sound of springs as he moved on the bed.

Her mother's voice, desperate: "Nothing," followed by a low keening sound. Then: "Could you hand it to me, the purse, please." Kara squeezed the knife handle. Her mother moved deeper into the room.

"What is going on here?"

"Give it to me! Let go of me!"

Kara jumped into the doorway, the knife thrust toward Chuck. "Let go of her."

Chuck's grip loosened. Her mother pulled free and ran

for the door, purse in hand. Kara backed out quickly, her eyes and the knife still pointed at him. He stood rigidly, paralyzed by confusion. "What's going on here?" he yelled. "What are you doing?"

They scrambled down the stairs. Out the front door. Her mother was already in the car when Kara cleared the front steps. She could hear Chuck behind her, screaming, "No. No. You can't go out there." Then she heard his footsteps on the stairs.

She jerked open the car door and her mother screamed, "Lock it, lock it." When she looked up he was there, his fingers splayed against the window, his face six inches from hers. "What the hell are you doing?" He pounded the old station wagon. "We're OK now. We've got the money. Where are you going?"

Her mother dug for the keys, found them, dropped them back into the purse. Found them again. She slipped them into place, twisted, and the engine caught. Chuck dashed to her window now, his T-shirt a blur of white in the growing light. "Gretchen, stop," he cried out. "Explain this to me."

Without a word, she put the car in gear.

"Don't go."

She gunned it in reverse.

"Oh God," he wailed, "don't leave me now."

# Art

*It's been so long I can't remember what it was about her.
Those slitty cat eyes? Her cheekbones? That streaky
blonde hair? That skinny little mink's body? That snarly
mouth? A quarter century of loving someone and now I
can't remember what I loved about her. I can remember
her leaning up against a freshly painted white wall at the
beginning of school one year. She was laughing with a
couple of her stupid girlfriends and I thought: Yes, I like
that one. But what was it?*

*The bitch.*

*She was so tiny, but she had so much pull. You could
be nowhere near her, then suddenly you'd fall into the
gravitational attraction of little planet Mary. And there
was no way to pull out.*

*I can remember this: her mouth was tipped up on one
side, snarly, cruel-and-amused-by-it, except when she
was in the back seat. We'd all be going somewhere and
I'd look back in the mirror and she'd be in the middle of*

*the seat, smiling at something, and I could see her. And her lips seemed balanced in the mirror.*

I don't think anyone ever got that close to her. She would stiff-arm you, keep you back, even while she was pulling you in. It was like she could suck you in without trying—it was a natural talent, like singing is for some people. She also knew how to pull herself back, but she wasn't as good at that. So she'd play around with it—pulling you in and then pulling herself away. Sport. And when she slipped up and you got right up next to her she'd do you, and that was a way of pushing you off again. For some women, sex is a way to create intimacy. For her, it was a way of diverting you so she could push you away again. A fuck-off.

I was too much of a chump to complain. Half a loaf and all. But if you thought about it, it would get to you. And I had time to think in the service. I got high like everyone else, but I paid serious attention to the big stuff. On the big stuff, I got more stand-up sober than I'd ever been in my life. I saw what I needed. Saw how it could work. She was married by then, but it didn't mean anything to her. You could see that. She was humping everyone on the island. You knew anything was possible on any given day. They weren't going to last.

And then she was gone.

*There's something cold about this: Everyone gets a shot at happiness when they are young and stupid, and everyone fucks it up. Some people get a chance to redeem themselves. They get to come through town twice. Like Heathcliff. Like that song about the guy nobody liked because he couldn't dance, and then he went away for a while, and when he came back, he was the best. He shut down all the other guys.*

*You go away. You come back. You got some money. You got some knowledge of the world. You got the pickup truck and the Purple Heart and the cold-blooded war stories. You are one very redeemed mannish boy. Watch me now!—but it doesn't matter. Before you know it, she's gone.*

*And the bitch of it is, she's still pulling you in. You're still falling toward the center even when there is no center there anymore.*

*So what are we talking about here? That once you fall in love, it takes over? That it becomes your destiny, your fate? That all the other stuff that should change the direction of your life—even that hellhole freak-show war—doesn't matter as much as love? And if it's your fate, if it's something you can't be released from . . . well, then. It changes things. It means you can't redeem yourself. This is your lot in life. You don't make the decisions anymore. You take your orders from love. Your job in life is to figure out what love wants you to do and then do it.*

*I have known what my love wants, ever since the cocksucker killed her. You cannot do that and not pay for it. I don't care if it's his fate or not. It's my fate to see him suffer. Whatever it takes. However long it takes.*

*If other people are harmed in this, maybe that's their fate. How the hell am I supposed to know? You can look at a person and see her twisted body in front of you and are you supposed to feel bad? Are you? And if you don't, does it mean you're crazy? And you didn't really understand your fate? And you've really fucked up?*

*I feel bad. I do. But it's not the kind of bad feeling I expected. Not what I've seen in the movies, anyway. Not like I felt in the war. This time, it's more like something leaked out of you and you're empty inside. It's bad enough. It's the end of my life, if I stop and think about it. I am truly and righteously fucked now, even if this works. But I can't say it hurts.*

*I can't remember how I got sucked into her, but I know why. I got sucked in because it made me feel so good. People make it out to be spiritual, but the fact is love is a good buzz. It makes you feel good. That's why you follow it. That's why you trust it even when you shouldn't. It makes you feel good. And then look what you do and look how it makes you feel. Look what you do to other people because of it. It degrades you and makes you hurt the people around you. It's not their fault. It's because love has this chokehold on you. And it keeps pulling you toward the heart of the hole.*

*If physics has meaning, then maybe all this gravity stops time. Or maybe you go through the hole and get time back again in a parallel existence. Or something like that.*

# Nineteen

He was tired, but couldn't sit. Couldn't stand still. He was cold, but he couldn't go inside. And he couldn't watch his wife and stepdaughter race away from him, so he paced the gravel driveway and wondered at their betrayal.

This was cataclysmic and unintelligible behavior—like an act of nature. All that supported them as a family had been destroyed. The pilings were gone. It could never, ever be rebuilt. But this was no random act. They had conspired against him. For what?

Some time after the station wagon had disappeared behind a curve of black pine trees and he was sure they were not coming back, he climbed the wooden steps and let himself inside.

The dining room looked blanched . . . the place mats

and throw rugs faded, the floor and cabinets and table washed out, monochromatic. This home was gone. His other home was gone. He would move now. He would live in the desert for a few years. Do penance in New Mexico. Or Tibet. He would go to the high, dry plains of Tibet and study the Book of the Dead.

No, he wouldn't. He would go to jail. They would tell about Mrs. Ford. They would get him convicted of that, even though he was blameless.

Out of the sameness before him, a single color arose, a harsh black quarter note of tar on the hardwood. Kara, he thought. Sweetheart. What happened down there? He saw another smear. And another. And others—a ragged composition that led to the basement door. He followed it there, and down.

The lightbulb was still glowing feebly. Nothing moved in the cool air, except the familiar musty vapors that rose up to greet him. Everything seemed familiar in this room— the creak of the stairs, the feeble light, the smell of wetness and decaying wood. And then something else.

At first he thought it was the roof tar, but he crouched to pick up the can and knew it was not that.

He thought: Garbage.

Then he turned his nose toward the little room under the stairs. The door was open only a few inches, but he could see the pale length of skin and knew she was there. He opened the door wider.

She looked awful. He stared at her, afraid to move, feeling the burn of the first tears. For a moment he was numb and then the anger raked through him. He felt sorrow at her death, but it was not as strong as his anger against the person who had killed her. The anger doubled when he grasped how the killer had destroyed her to attack him. Had arranged her in this way so that others would attack him with special vengeance, special vigor. He knew she would be outraged at the degradation, at being displayed like that. He regretted now that he had not been more gentle with the older woman's corpse, that he had not treated it with more respect. Even after the soul was gone, something of the person was still attached to the body; he knew because that remnant of Jeanine had been so coldly violated by this killer.

The tears came more easily now, without burning. He took her hand and leaned for a second against the woodpile next to her, planning what he would do. He would have to call Lyle in Bayfield. He would explain everything and ask for advice. Lyle would be back in an hour at most. Then it would start up, but he would be protected from the worst of them. He would hope for the best. But of course Gretchen and Kara would talk about Mrs. Ford, and the best would be grim.

When he could not bear to see her anymore, he looked away, out of the little room, and saw the heavy footprints that moved toward the beach door. Kara had not made those, and neither he nor Gretchen had been tracking around tar.

His spirits lifted. The tar had been knocked over when the killer dumped the body here. He had walked through it, stupid with haste and fear. Had felt the pull of it and run faster, not looking down. Had left a signature that a good cop could read. A good cop would find the boots— would find a nick in the sole, a wear pattern, something to brand the murderer.

Chuck rose immediately, carefully, thinking now that his future might depend on not stepping in the roof cement, not touching the doorknob, not disturbing the thousand delicate clues around him.

He looked back at Jeanine, then reached down and closed her eyes. Pulled down her sweater. Straightened her damp skirt. Apologized.

Upstairs, he punched in Lyle's number. He got a single busy signal, followed by three distorted chimes. A garbled recording informed him that his call could not go through. He slammed down the phone and dialed again. This time he tried to reach the Bayfield police, since Lyle might be already on his way to get a search warrant.

He got the chimes again. The freezing rain had screwed up the lines somehow.

He tried the operator. Maybe she could connect him with Lyle. Or maybe Art. If Lyle was gone, Gretchen and Kara would go to Art. He'd shown them the house when they first drove out from the ferry. He'd insist that the operator stay on the line until he reached someone.

He got a ring. And another. He took a tumbler out of the cupboard

(. . . *three . . . four . . .*)

and poured in a half shot of CC. He stared out the window to the lake, out the other window to the woodshed,

(. . . *seven . . . eight . . .*)

out the door to the dining room and living room and the tarry tracks that ran from the kitchen to the stairs . . . and then another set of faint tracks that he hadn't noticed before, that ran from the front door to the kitchen and then to

(. . . *ten . . .*)

the lion-foot chair near the stove. And back out.

He hung up. He put down the glass, and moved quickly to the chair even though he knew that what he was seeing wouldn't change up close. He bent down, touched the tar, brought it to his nostrils so that he could smell it and make himself sure.

He was sure.

Kara had walked directly from the basement upstairs; he could track her steps. Only Art had sat in Leo's chair, for an instant, after Blaylock had threatened him.

If you get a chance, this is what you tell Lyle, he thought. You say Jeanine's body is in the basement. You say you think your oldest friend killed her and put her there. He walked through tar on his way out, and the traces were still on his boots two hours later when he came back with you and Brian and Blaylock.

You don't know why he killed her—anger, jealousy, accident. You do know he wanted people to find her there. Because he started waving around hundred-dollar bills trying to get people to come here, ransack this place, find her body.

Chuck thought: You think you know why, but you don't need to say so right now. Art must have known all along. From Leo, maybe, but more likely he had figured it out on his own. He had been there when they brought her through the hole in the ice, had seen the watch on her, had noticed it missing, had filled in the other details. And now Gretchen and Kara were probably fleeing to him.

He tried dialing Lyle again, heard the chimes. Hung up. There was no one left to call. No other help. He took the heaviest jacket he could find—Leo's old parka—from the hooks by the back door and pulled on his running shoes.

This is the way Leo saw the world, he thought. No great canopy of civil authority over you. A couple of public servants to handle a few communal tasks, but for the most part, you took care of your own shit.

The key to the old Triumph was hanging from a nail behind the woodshed door.

# Twenty

## 5:15 A.M.

Gretchen had to fight herself not to speed. Speed hardly mattered now. He was stuck back at the house, and even though he might run—into the woods, into one of the summer cabins, down the highway after her and Kara—he would not be able to cover the fifteen miles into town. Not before dawn. Not before she had found Lyle or Art or someone, anyone, even Gromek, even Bartok.

She sped past a rusty black pickup parked at the side of the road and thought she saw a form slumped inside it. She drove on: it might have been someone watching the house, but she couldn't tell who. She was sure it wasn't Lyle or Art, and they were the only ones she trusted.

The drizzle had turned briefly to sleet. Now a light fili-gree of snow danced in the beam of the headlights, fell to the pavement, slicked it. She was moving too fast. They were safe now.

Kara was the next priority. "We're OK now, honey," she told her daughter. "We're going to find someone to get us off the island and he'll never find us again. He won't be able to get off the island on his own because he's afraid of the water. They'll track him and catch him. He's not a danger to us now. Do you understand?"

The girl pressed herself into the car seat, arms crossed tightly across her chest. "You can't imagine what she looked like, Mom. She was still wet. He drowned her and then propped her up like she was some kind of inflatable sex toy."

Gretchen shuddered. "He'll pay for that. You saw these people. You saw what they think of him. He'll be lucky if they just kill him outright."

"You know how weird it was that he took his boots off outside?" Kara said. "It was because when he brought her into the basement, he knocked over a can of this roofing cement. Black, tarry stuff. And he walked through it, you could see the footprints right in it. He knew it. He didn't have time to clean them off, so he left them outside."

Gretchen wanted to reply, wanted to keep talking, to keep the line open to Kara. But her mind drifted, searching.

He had killed Mrs. Ford and buried her in the woods. He had killed Jeanine, but instead of hiding her, he dragged the body into the house while she and her daughter slept and *arranged* her under the stairs. It was like the one body didn't matter to him and the other one did. She shivered. And then he left her there. Did he want her to be found after they were gone? They would go looking for him then, so he must have been planning to disappear.

What does that tell you? she thought. What was he planning to do with you?

She could say none of this to Kara, so she said, "We should try to find Lyle first, but he might have gone over to Bayfield. If he's not at home, we'll find Art."

"But he's Chuck's friend."

"Yes, but that won't matter now. If we tell him what we know, he'll help us. He'll help us contact Lyle."

Lyle's driveway and front lawn were lit by a white mercury lamp hung from the top of a telephone pole planted in the center of the yard. It was the only light except for a pale orange glow behind the doorbell. Gretchen pressed the button, saw the orange light go out, released and pressed again, longer this time. The wind whipped the snow, tossed the tree branches, then stopped. There was no car in the driveway and the open garage was filled with the shadows of garden tools and old appliances. When she opened the screen door, the hinges screeched in the crisp silence. She looked back, worried that Chuck might somehow appear. She knocked hard four times and four again, in quick succession. No response.

She climbed back into the warm car and locked the door again. She slammed it into gear and cut a half-circle across the lawn toward the highway.

Art's house was another couple of miles toward town. "He's going to be home," Gretchen said confidently. "He's going to be sleeping and we'll wake him up and it will be fine."

"He has the motorcycle," Kara said suddenly. She sat up straight, then looked out the wagon's back window. "Chuck has the bike, in the woodshed, and he knows how to ride it."

Gretchen glanced up immediately into the rearview

mirror. "He won't know where to find us. He can't . . . I don't think he wants us, anyway. He wants to get away, right?"

"You can't know what he wants," Kara said flatly.

She was already past the driveway when she recognized Art's unlit house. She jerked on the brakes, backed up in two reckless swerves, then pulled into the driveway. As she clambered out of the car this time, Kara came along. She rang the doorbell and her daughter pounded the door and no one answered.

"Come on," said Kara. "Come on."

No one answered.

Then they heard the growl of an engine and the whine of tires on the highway. Kara yelled, "Get in the car," and when the high beams swung off the road and up the driveway, the light showed them snatching at the doors of the station wagon.

Kara's back was turned, so she didn't know it was Art until Gretchen said, "Stop. Stop. It's him." She waved and ran to his truck. Art and Brian were climbing out the door before it had fully stopped.

"What's the matter? What's going on?"

Gretchen let herself cry now and fell against him. "Oh, Art. He did it. He killed them."

"Killed who?" Art asked.

"Mary. Jeanine. And probably . . ."

"Na-not Chuck," Brian interrupted.

Kara took a step toward them and stopped. "We have to get inside your house now," she said. "He might be coming after us."

Art's eyes flicked between them. "Did . . . does he have a gun or anything?"

Kara: "I don't know. But we have to get inside."

He unlocked the front door and urged them to go in. Gretchen stopped in the dark living room, smelled the dust and mildew of it, noted the old couch and recliner, the TV on the coffee table. He left them, ran up the narrow stairway. "Brian, lock the door," he called back. "And leave the lights off. I don't want him to be able to see us in here."

Brian locked the door, then shuffled to the bottom of the stairs, waiting. He turned nervously toward Kara, but didn't lift his eyes. When Art came back, he had a rifle and shells in his hand. "We should move your car. Hide it. But first, tell me what happened."

"Kara found her. Found Jeanine's body in the basement."

"She was wet," Kara said.

"And there's more." Gretchen hesitated. This was opening a terrible chasm, but she wanted to reveal all she knew now. "I think he killed Mary. And he might have killed Mrs. Ford too. Drowned her."

"What?" Brian's voice cracked.

Gretchen said, "He was chasing her and she fell in the water. He claimed. Maybe he pushed her. I don't know. But he wouldn't let us tell anyone, because they would think he did it on purpose. Oh, Jesus." She sobbed again.

"She's buried in the woods," Kara said.

"Oh, Jesus." Art paced away from them, toward the kitchen, then back. "You mean he killed her? Mrs. Ford? Why the hell would he do that?"

"She was trying to run away with Leo's diary," Gretchen replied. "He thought maybe there was something in it about the money. I don't know. She might have fallen. I don't know."

"The crazy son of a bitch."

"I can't believe this," Brian said. He chewed on the corner of his mouth. "Something is wrong."

Gretchen turned to Art. "I know he was your friend."

"The son of a bitch. You're absolutely sure about Mrs. Ford?"

"No," Kara snapped. "We're not sure at all. But we're sure about Jeanine. We just went to Lyle's and he's not there. Can you please help us find him?"

He didn't respond immediately. "Lyle's not around. He's still on the mainland and the phones are all fucked up with this storm."

"Isn't someone else an acting deputy?" Gretchen asked. "I mean, who's in charge when Lyle's gone?"

"Bartok." Art hesitated.

"Do something," Kara implored. "He's got that motorcycle. He might be coming here now. He might be just down the road right now."

"OK, OK." Art still hesitated.

"Call Bartok," Gretchen said. "Let's get some more people in on this."

Kara agreed. "Let's get them all. Go to town and get as many as we can and at least be ready for him if he shows up."

Art shook his head. "No good. Half the guys in town were on a bender last night, Bartok included. They're all sleeping it off now."

"They wouldn't be a help," Brian said.

Art picked up the shells and began to slip them into the chamber. "Even when they're sober, you can't trust them. That's what scared me earlier. I was afraid that if they found something at Leo's, they might disturb the evidence. They might give him a loophole if it was an illegal search. We want to do this right. By the book. So this is what we do. We run down to my sailboat and raise the Bayfield Coast Guard on the marine radio. They can contact Lyle in five minutes. Twenty minutes later he'll be over here in the sheriff's speedboat."

For the first time in twelve hours, Gretchen felt like things were coming under control. "Yes. Yes, that's good," she said.

Art led the way out the back door, holding the rifle chest high, in both hands. It was colder and the snow was falling more thickly but she was glad, needed the icy chill on her cheeks to stay awake and alert. He said, "Brian, you lead the way. I'll guard the rear."

They moved quickly down the rocky path, their footsteps muffled by pine needles. Through the snow, Gretchen could see the water casting up bright fragments of light, reflections of Bayfield's streetlamps and porch lights across the channel. The chilled piney air made her shiver over and over. She could hear no sounds except the lapping water, the hoarse sigh of the trees.

They passed a large granite outcropping and the path ended abruptly at a metal dock with a long white sailboat tied up to it. "Get on," Art said, and she and her daughter quickly straddled the vinyl-covered safety lines and hopped into the cockpit. He followed, never taking his eyes off the path. In a swift motion, he pushed back the companionway hatch. "Unless he's got a gun, you're OK here," he said. "He'd rather turn himself in than step on board a sailboat. Let's go below, try to reach Lyle. Brian, you go back to the crest, there. Watch for him and if he shows, give a holler. You OK doing that?"

"No problem." He stood on the dock a moment, looking up at the stars. "We should have moved their car."

"It's too late for that now. Just go watch for him while I call Lyle."

Gretchen followed Kara into the dark cabin. Art came last, the rifle thunking against the sides of the companionway. He flipped a small switch, and weepy light illuminated the cabin. Dirty dishes sat in the metal sink. Old clothes were strewn on the settees.

Art flipped another switch and static spilled from the radio. He pulled the handset from a hook and spoke: "Coast Guard. Coast Guard. This is the *Chinook II* from Madeline with an emergency call for Bayfield Coast Guard. Do you read me? Over."

He released the talk button and listened, his eyes trained on the empty space over Gretchen's shoulder.

No answer.

Gretchen, too, stared into space, waiting, but Kara suddenly clutched her arm.

She glanced at her daughter, then followed her eyes to the small glob of tar smeared across the slats at their feet. Her glance rose sharply to Art, then caught another, fainter stain on the companionway step, three inches from her resting hand. She gasped and jerked her hand away.

Art frowned at her, then repeated his call: "Coast Guard, do you read me? This is the *Chinook II*." He released the talk button but this time his eyes fell directly on the black mark. He rubbed a finger over it, felt it, swore. He looked down absently, saw the mark on the floor. Lifted his boot, inspected the bottom. Swore again.

Then he caught the terror in Kara's eyes.

The raspy male voice came over the speaker.

"*Chinook II, Chinook II*. This is Bayfield Coast Guard, switch to Channel 56 immediately."

At first he didn't move. Then he spun in the channel and pressed the button. His eyes stayed fixed on Kara. "Coast Guard, this is Art Sannar on *Chinook II*. I need to contact Lyle Pointer immediately, on a police matter. He went over there a couple of hours ago. I think he's working with the Bayfield police. I'd call him there, but our phones are down. I know it's not your job, but could you call around? See if you could find him, and then ask him to radio me?"

The radio operator pressed for more details, but Art said only that he'd explain everything to Lyle. And then he hung the handset back on its hook.

His eyes had never moved off Kara.

"What's the matter with you?"

"Nothing."

"Look, I know you're under a lot of stress. But this is no time to go south on me. There's no telling what he's up to. I think we need to communicate, don't you?"

"It's nothing," Gretchen said. She tried to bluff: "Somehow, when you called the Coast Guard and everything, it made it all seem real. This whole nightmare."

He nodded slowly, then snarled. "Don't bullshit me." He grabbed Kara roughly by the arm. "Talk," he ordered.

"Stop, please."

"Leave her alone," Gretchen yelled.

"What's going on?" he demanded.

"You're hurting me!" Kara planted her feet and pulled away, toward the bow. He stepped with her and she yelled, "Mom, go!" and Gretchen leaped for the stairs, but not to run. She braced herself to kick out at him, but his thick arm caught her first, and spun her around. She went down on one knee, sprawling over the settee bench, and Kara screamed.

"What the hell is going on?" he demanded. "Are you trying to bring Chuck down here? Are you in this with him?"

Kara and Gretchen looked at each other. Neither spoke. Quietly Kara said, "I'm not afraid of Chuck. He didn't do anything."

"What're you talking about? Two minutes ago he was Charles Manson."

He was not buying the bluff, and she was so disgusted by him that she could not restrain herself. It didn't matter, anyway. Soon, everyone would know what she knew. "You did it."

"I what?"

"You killed Jeanine and it's obvious, which means you're fucked. You left a trail of tar from her body to here. It's on the ladder. It's in your truck, your house, everywhere you went tonight."

He swore and pounded his fist against the companionway ladder.

Kara leaned toward him. "You're busted."

He hit her so hard her head snapped back, then she slammed into the bulwark and collapsed. Gretchen was beside her instantly, holding her daughter's head.

"You don't talk to me like that, little girl." Art picked up the rifle and pointed it at them. "Don't move." He leaped out of the cabin in two steps, then she heard him running across the deck—first toward the bow, then back into the cockpit.

Kara said "I'm OK" twice before Gretchen believed her. Then she took her daughter's head in her hands and whispered to her. "Get back in there, in the front. There might be a way out, a hatch overhead. Get ready to run for it. I'm going to try the radio."

"No," she began, but Gretchen shook her, saying, "He's going to cast off. Go now. Now."

She let go of her daughter and ran to the radio. She fumbled with the handset, trying to get it off the hook, but before she got it free she heard Kara cry out, and then the simultaneous crack on her skull and the flash of pain. Instantly Kara was at her side. Her vision was blurred, but she couldn't tell if it was from a concussion or the pain.

His voice growled above them. "Nothing cute." He reached into the cabin, unplugged the handset from the radio, and disappeared again behind the wheel. The next sound Gretchen could make out was a high whine, followed by the grumbling of a diesel engine. The cabin began to vibrate, at first gently, then with force as the boat pulled away from the dock. "The hatch," she whispered to Kara. "Call for Brian. Swim for it if you can."

Gretchen pulled herself up, her head still thick with the blow he had given her. She braced herself on the companionway ladder, trying to block his sight, and stared up at him. There was enough pale light to see now, but his face was blocked by the wheel.

"You are going to kill us now," she said. "I understand that. But I have one favor . . . please kill my daughter first." She was talking crazy now but knew she had to keep it going. "I don't want her to see me die. It's the only thing I can do for her now."

His voice was icy. "If you want to do something for her, go back into the V-berth and tell her that I can't quite get the hatch in my sights. The mast will cover her. But as soon as she moves her head two inches on either side of the mast, I'll blow it off. OK? I'm cocking the gun right now."

She heard the metallic click and tried to yell over the

engine noise, then was afraid that Kara wouldn't hear her. She staggered back, screaming again and again. "Stop. Don't try to run. Stop."

Above her, Kara yelled out, "Brian, Brian, help! Help!"

He cut the engine, and in the silence that followed, his voice was clipped and unmistakable. "Don't do that. You're going to be responsible if anything happens to him."

"Brian!"

She could hear his feet hammering onto the metal dock. "Art. Art. Where are you going?"

Kara yelled back. "He's taking us away to kill us, Brian."

"Art, what are you doing? You can't protect him like that." He was pacing frantically at the end of the dock. "Everyone will know he did it. You can't hurt them."

"Don't you worry about anything, Brian. They don't understand. I'm not going to hurt them."

"He is!" Kara screamed. "Help us."

"You come back, Art. Come back now."

In reply, Art re-hit the starter on the inboard. It coughed twice but didn't catch. In the instant before he hit the button again, she heard the splash and then Art swore. "Go back, Brian. You'll freeze." There was no answer. The starter coughed and died.

Kara said, "I'm going to go for it." She had squeezed most of her trunk through the hatch when the first shot rang out. When Gretchen heard it scream by, she grabbed her daughter's legs and pulled her back belowdecks. "Are you hurt?" she cried. "Are you hurt?"

"No. No. I'm OK," Kara gasped. "I'm OK."

There was a moment of absolute silence then. He was not moving above them and he was not trying to restart the engine. A single shot exploded. Another second of silence. Then the grind of the starter. This time it caught.

"Oh, Jesus," Gretchen said. "He shot him."

In a few moments, they were two hundred yards from shore. The boat pitched violently as it broke through the wave peaks and slid down into the troughs. He eased off the throttle. Gretchen worked her way to the companionway, not sure of what he was doing or what she would do next. She couldn't see his face. She was still searching when he spoke.

"That was hard to do," he said. "I think it was a mistake, but I didn't know what else to do."

He pulled his pipe and pouch out of his jacket, filled the pipe and lit it. "I'm not as bad as you think." He coughed once. "Jeanine . . . Jeanine was more or less a suicide. She was never in the best psychological condition, you know. Always carried a crush on someone—your husband, Donny Gromek, me. For some reason, though, she really thought Chuck would come back and take her away from old Blaylock. Until she saw you two, I don't think it really hit her."

Another cough, then: "I didn't plan to do anything when I went to your house. Then when I went downstairs for the wine I thought: What the hell. Unlock the basement door, man. Maybe you'll want to come back and kill the prick in his sleep.

"I might have done it too. But then she showed up at my place a half hour after I got home. Hysterical. Started in about how she hated her life. How she'd worked her way down the food chain of love until she'd hit Wilkerson, and now he was losing interest.

"She was so miserable and she knew I couldn't bear that. She knew I'd help her. I got her drunk. Gave her some Valium. More drinks, more Valium. When she got real wobbly I brought her down to the lake and she pretty much killed herself."

Kara sobbed. Gretchen stared up at the faint orange glow of the pipe, smelled the sweet tobacco. "You killed her," she said.

He took a deep drag on the pipe and exhaled calmly. Another whiff of sweet smoke, then: "She killed herself. I just made it easy. Then I tied her around Chuck's neck because it made sense. Balance. Hey, you know, when I carried her into the basement, the jerk was outside digging through the woodshed. I was fifty feet away from him and he never knew I was there."

"And I bought it," Gretchen said bitterly.

"Oh, you were buying a line of bullshit long before I came into the picture, lady. You bought it the first time you slept with him. When you married him. When you let your daughter live in the same house with that twisted son of a bitch. He killed Mary, you know. He waited until I was away in the service and then he married her and then . . . when I got back . . . he killed her. He did a good job of making it look like she got drunk and drove through the ice, but he never fooled me. So you see the balance here. He got away with that one, but he's going to get stuck with Jeanine."

"Wrong," she said. "You are going to get caught for that and Brian and for anything you do to us. You don't think anyone will wonder why our station wagon is in your front yard? What kind of story do you think you can use to cover that? And how about the tracks? You walked right through the roof cement. You can wash and wash your carpet, but they'll find traces of it. There and in your truck."

"I was the one who found the hole she went through," he said. "It was New Year's and I was going over to Bayfield to a party and I saw the car tracks going off the road and the damn hole. I saw all that and I saw footprints coming back from where he'd turned off the ice road. But they were gone by the time I got back with the police. Blown away. Covered with snow. I tried to explain to the cops but I wasn't very coherent, I suppose. I was wasted pretty much twenty-four hours a day at that time in my life.

"I was there when the divers went down and I saw them bring her up and she had the watch on. She had a watch on but she didn't have it on after Leo had blessed her body. They said it never existed, but I know what I saw. I saw the tracks. I saw the watch. I saw that Chuck was mourning her and relieved at the same time and then he left town."

She looked away for an instant and saw that Kara had stopped sobbing; she had found a small kitchen knife in the sink. She had set it aside and was now gently prying the fire extinguisher from its holder near the radio.

Gretchen moved up a step, trying again to fill his vision. "We won't come out of here. You'll have to drag us out and we'll fight. Our blood will be all over and they will find it, identify it. Our hair." She took a handful and pulled, crying out, then showed him what she had harvested. "See this?" She dropped it to the floor of the cabin. "They'll find that too. You'll clean and clean and they only need to find one hair, one drop of blood."

Art knocked the pipe against the side of the sailboat, letting the ashes drop into the water. Then he shifted the rifle in his arms. "He told you he acted crazy for his draft board, didn't he? He told everyone that. The truth was he was always out of his fucking head. He never had to make up anything."

"You're crazy."

He set the rifle down and revved the engine again. "I'm going to see he gets what's coming to him. The great thing about justice is that you can put it off and put it off and it's still good. It has a long shelf life.

"But you two—I can't explain you away. Can I? There's going to be no justice in killing you. It's going to be really unfair."

# Twenty-one

### 5:30 A.M.

The speed felt unmanageable, as though he were constantly in the first stage of a long skid, about to tip onto his side and leave a trail of skin and clothing. He reacted, overcompensated, nearly dumping the bike on the other side, reacted again, weaving uncertainly toward the village.

By the first curve, behind the pines, he felt like he had conquered the worst fear, which was that he could not master the first elements of riding the motorcycle. He could sit straight on it. Could see through the thin flakes of snow that stung his face. Could lean slightly with the sweep of the highway. He would not self-destruct.

The rest of it—the slick wet pavement, the balky gears, the arctic wind that pierced his thin gloves and made his hands crab over the bars as though they would never be pried free—all that remained out of his control. He was still terrified, but in the hierarchy of his fears, this was far down the list. He feared for Gretchen and Kara; he feared for himself if he failed them.

The cold burned his hands. He told himself that the distances could be measured in minutes. Ten to Lyle's place. Fifteen to Art's. Twenty to town.

At the last curve before Lyle's, he tried to throttle back but had trouble getting his hand to do the work. When he finally was able to release the throttle and squeeze the brake, he had shot past the driveway. He pulled over and looked back, seeing immediately that the house was dark. Lyle was gone, and no Subaru in the driveway. He worked his hands off the bars, and held them for a moment under the parka, until he could feel the blood needling through them again. Then he drew them out, kicked the bike into gear.

He was sure they were at Art's. His plan was to stop before he got to the house, then walk up. This would give him the advantage of surprise, as well as functioning hands. But as he approached Art's driveway, he saw a flicker of taillights a hundred yards down the road. He was sure it was a pickup, guessed it was Art's. Who else would be on the road at this hour? He wouldn't be alone either; he was taking Kara and Gretchen with him.

Chuck shot past the driveway and twisted the throttle forward.

The truck was making time, inching away from him. He bent lower over the bars—partly for speed, partly to escape the frigid gale that tore at his face. Still the truck pulled away. Glimpses of the taillights through the pine trees and brush were fewer, of shorter duration. The snow was thicker now. It burned his cheeks and clung to his eyes and greased the surface of the road.

Abruptly, the truck pulled over.

He had trouble stopping again. The pain shot through his hand and up his wrist and arm. He managed to ease off the gas but he couldn't grip the brake with enough force. The bike gradually ran down but he was still going twenty miles an hour when he reached the truck, which was black, not orange like Art's, and which held not Kara and Gretchen but a man, visible as he opened the cab door, the better to view the winter cyclist who was approaching.

Blaylock, stupid with liquor and melancholy, stepped out onto the highway. Chuck swerved around him, heard him yell. He felt the bike begin to slide, then miraculously right itself.

He stopped, wondering what Blaylock had yelled, wondering if he knew something about Gretchen and Kara. When Blaylock scrambled into his truck, Chuck expected that he was going to drive up to him. Instead, the disheveled little man climbed back out of the truck, this time holding a rifle. He bellowed at Chuck, raised the rifle too quickly, and fell on the snow-slicked highway. As he scrambled to get up, his flailing legs kicked the rifle under his truck.

Chuck gunned the Triumph and drove off as quickly as he dared. He was on the outskirts of the village now, speeding past one house, then several. He was going in the wrong direction but couldn't think of a way to get past Blaylock. He thought he heard the crack of the rifle and gunned the motor. In the vibrating mirror, Blaylock's truck seemed not to be moving. Another crack.

He gunned the bike again, and this time lost control. The wheels spun in the snow and then suddenly caught, lurching ahead and then across the road, throwing him forward over the handlebars into the ditch. He heard the thud as he hit. The Triumph followed, rolled over his leg, and fell into a small pine tree. A fine mist of powdery snow exploded around him.

Chuck lay flat, grunting and gasping. He twisted his head, looking back for Blaylock.

A loud crack echoed down the highway. He heard the ping of the bullet bouncing off the pavement somewhere ahead of him. Then another crack and ping, this one close to him on the left.

He didn't see Blaylock climb back into the truck, but he heard the gears grind. The truck's high beams flashed on, and the sound of the approaching truck swelled quickly. He pushed himself up on his elbows, then dropped flat when he heard Blaylock fire another round. The drunk was driving at him, accelerating, hanging out the window, squeezing off shots.

Chuck looked toward the woods, then back, then saw the truck start to skid. The front wheels drifted right while the rear wheels seemed to pull out on the left, as if trying to pass. Soon the truck was gliding sideways down the road, Blaylock still leaning out the window, firing straight over the truck's front fender as it turned a sliding circle on the highway—his shots hammering into the ditch, into the woods, now backward up the road, now in the opposite ditch above Chuck's head.

The truck seemed to be still accelerating when it plowed sideways into the woods fifty yards back from Chuck. There was a crash, then silence. Then an explosion as the truck caught fire, sending a ball of black-edged flames into the bare, crowning branches of a large maple.

Another explosion followed. Gas or chemicals in the truck bed, Chuck guessed. The heat rolled over him.

He stood, tested the leg the bike had run over. It was

stiff but he could walk on it. The bike had not fared as well—the front tire was flat, the handlebars twisted. He glanced once more at the burning truck and then turned toward the village, hoping for a sign that Lyle had returned from Bayfield.

There was nothing. Full light was still a half hour off, but the night was quickly seeping away. His eyes swept the deserted main street, the faces of the darkened buildings. The marina parking lot was empty, and the lot near the ferry pier. A small van was parked at the end of the pier, though, off to the side of the ferry's huge gates. Then he noticed the faint light in the cabin. The first crossing was still an hour or two away, but Gromek or one of his boys might be up there getting ready. Maybe someone slept on the ferry.

In any case, there would be a radio. He would contact Lyle on the mainland, then take the van and go after Gretchen and Kara.

With his hands still tucked in the front of his parka, he jogged down the hill and onto the pier. The farther he got from the land, the stronger the light became, and the fresher the breeze.

"Hello, hello," he yelled. "Anyone up there?"

No answer.

"Gromek? Anyone?"

Still no answer. A set of two oil-stained wooden steps stood off to the side of the gate. When Chuck mounted them, he saw that another set of steps led down on the other side of the gate. Careful to keep his eyes on the cabin light and not on the water, he threw one leg over the swaying gate, then heaved himself over the top. His foot missed the top step, and his hands, still half numb, lost their hold and he slipped. For one eternal moment he was sure he was falling into the water, to drown or be crushed between the boat and the concrete pier. When he crashed onto the thick steel deck of the ferry, the pain in his hands made him stiffen and then crawl into a fetal ball—but he was not in the water.

"Hold it there." Gromek's voice was nervous, even higher than usual. Chuck heard his steps ringing down the metal stairs from the cabin. He looked up, and in the mounting light he saw the old man dressed in coveralls and a heavy wool plaid jacket. The pistol in his left hand was not pointed at Chuck, but Gromek kept enough room between them so he could point and fire if need be.

"Have you gone completely nuts? Get the hell off my boat."

"Please." Chuck pulled himself slowly into a crouch, then stood. "I found Jeanine. In the basement at the house. She's dead."

Gromek's face fell. "Oh, no."

"Art did it. I don't know why. But he did it."

"Art? You come in here and expect me to believe that Art killed Jeanine?" Gromek's mouth twitched and now he raised the pistol toward Chuck. "Let's just come along and we'll radio Lyle. This is his business."

Chuck shook his head. "You go ahead. Tell him I've gone to find Gretchen and Kara. They freaked out when they saw Jeanine. They thought I did it and they drove off and I'm afraid they ran to Art. I have to find them. I need your van."

Gromek stepped aside and waved the gun from Chuck to the stairs. "You're not going anywhere, except with me. The thought of shooting Leo's boy should pain me, but the honest truth is I'd enjoy it, God help me. Now move."

"No way. I'm going after my wife and daughter."

"I will not let you go hunt down another woman, mister." For the first time he leveled the gun, aimed it with purpose at Chuck's chest. "I will shoot you dead first. Don't give me an excuse."

Chuck knew that old Gromek *would* shoot him, probably with pleasure. "I have to find them. Don't try to keep me here."

"One misstep and I'll drop you. Am I being clear?"

The old captain was not bluffing. Chuck put his head in his tortured hands and surrendered. He stood, and Gromek followed him up the stairs, four steps back. When Chuck reached the warm, sleep-musty pilothouse, the old man told him to step back all the way to the far windows. He did what he was told.

Gromek took the handset off the side of the radio and pressed the talk button. "Bayfield Coast Guard. Coast Guard. This is the ferry *Intrepid*, hailing the Bayfield Coast Guard. Over." The radio crackled with instructions to switch channels and when Gromek did, the first voice he heard was Lyle's. "Hey, what the hell is going on over there? These guys got a call from Art, but now I can't seem to raise him. Over."

Chuck focused on the low ceiling of the pilothouse, trying to figure out what Art could have wanted, thinking it was probably a good sign. If you were in the process of killing someone, you wouldn't call the police.

"This is what we've got. Chuck says he's found Jeanine's body. Says she's dead and claims Art killed her. I don't believe him. His wife and the kid ran off because they don't believe him either. They might be with Art. Unless you believe him, I wouldn't worry about them.

I've got Chuck with me now, on the boat. I've got a gun and he's not going anywhere. Over."

"You've got a gun? Over."

"Yes. And you don't have to worry about me. Over."

"Jesus, Gromek, please don't shoot anyone. I'm on my way. I'll be there in fifteen minutes. Just stay put and please don't shoot anyone. Over."

"I hear you." He smiled at the deputy's discomfort, but in the next instance he glanced over Chuck's shoulder and his amusement withered. He squinted, then frowned. "And say, Lyle, you might try raising Art again. I think I see his boat is heading up the channel. Over."

Chuck spun around to see the boat, its sails still covered, motoring along the shore. A half mile away, in the early light, its hull was the color of parchment.

"Thanks. You figure he's headed this way? Over."

"Negative. He's heading up-channel, toward the lake. Hanging in close to shore. Over."

"I'll give him a holler. Over and out."

"I told you," Chuck said.

"Shut up." Gromek spun the dial back to the hailing frequency and they both listened as Lyle called out to Art: "*Chinook II. Chinook II.* This is Bayfield Coast Guard calling *Chinook II.* Art? Can you hear me? Over." A flare of static followed while Lyle waited for Art to reply. Then Lyle again: *"Chinook II. Chinook II . . ."*

Chuck stared at the receding fiberglass hull. "He's running away."

"He's motoring his boat," Gromek spit back, but his voice was strained. "He knows he couldn't run away from anything in that boat."

"He's got Gretchen and Kara and he's a killer."

"Listen, kiddo. Don't get worked up, because you are not going anywhere until Lyle gets here. And then you'll be lucky if you . . ."

The sound of the air horn pierced the dawn.

"There!" Chuck yelled. "They're trying to get help." The air horn continued to blare, then was muffled. Then silence.

"Don't get jumpy on me," Gromek said. "You hear. Don't make me nervous." The old man picked up the handset again. "Lyle. You hear that?"

Chuck saw the two large clouds of smoke rise in the cockpit, then a smaller puff. Then the sailboat disappeared around an outcropping. "Look," he cried. "Did you see that? It's on fire."

"Lyle, did you read me? Over."

The radio crackled, then Lyle's voice: "What's going on over there?"

Gromek was agitated now. He flicked a switch on the control panel, then another. "I heard what sounded like a distress call on an air horn, but I'm not sure. Also saw what looked to be smoke." The big engines of the ferry kicked in. "I'm going after him. Over."

"We're right behind you. Over."

Gromek put the gun in the pocket of his coat and turned to go. "I'll be throwing off the lines now," he said. "Don't touch anything. And don't try to fuck around with me, kid. I'd hate to have to shoot you and then find out you weren't the complete son of a bitch I think you are. I'd hate that like hell."

"We're going after them." Chuck's lips tightened strangely over his teeth.

Gromek stopped, stared at him coldly. "Would you get off if I let you off?"

Chuck shook his head. "No way. This . . ."

"No way what?"

He screamed it: "Go! Just go!"

# Twenty-two

**6:15 A.M.**

He dived down the companionway, pushing Gretchen aside, and wrestled the air horn from Kara. When he spun around, Gretchen was ready for him. She raised the fire extinguisher and blasted his face. The hiss and the blinding clouds of vapor filled the room for an instant and then she heard him scream. Kara had stabbed him with the kitchen knife. She sprayed his face again and he flailed at her, one arm smashing across her shoulder. She couldn't see what happened next, but she heard a crash and Kara yelled, "The knife!"

Gretchen swung the canister blindly through the cloud, aiming high in case Kara was close. "Get the gun," she yelled. In an instant, the cloud began dissipating, and she could see Art grappling with her daughter as she tried to climb out of the cabin. Gretchen swung at him again, the blow landing across his neck. He grunted, but didn't turn

236

back. He and Kara spilled into the cockpit together, but he reached the rifle first. Gretchen didn't see where her daughter went, but she followed Art, blasted him again. In the next instant, his hand was on her neck.

He dropped the rifle and used that hand to force her arm back until it was laid out against the deck. The pressure on her neck was building. She clenched the extinguisher with all her strength but he ripped it out of her grip. The small canister fit neatly into his hand, like an oversized truncheon, and he swung it at her head. It struck her raised arm with such excruciating pain that she was sure the arm was broken. He swung again and this time the blow glanced off her face. She screamed and slid to the wooden slats on the cockpit deck. Above her, she heard Kara's footfalls, her voice yelling, "Mom! Mom!"

He was at the wheel. She heard him cursing. She had no idea where the boat had motored during the melee. She turned her head but could not see over the side of the cockpit. The snow fell thickly on her, forming a slush between the wooden slats. She could see Art now. Blood covered one of his hands. The rifle was in his good hand, pointed at her head.

"OK, you little bitch," he yelled at Kara. "This is what happens. I'm going to put a bullet into your mother's gut and you can listen to her for a while. How's that sound?"

Kara didn't answer.

"You don't get it. You can't hide behind the mast on a sailboat. I could shoot you dead right now if I wanted to. But I want you to hear her dying first. That's what you get for cutting me."

Kara's voice came back strong over the growl of the engine. "People are going to see you, chump. People will hear the gun. You're going to kill us both, but it only means you'll pay a higher price."

"I don't think so. No one will see much in this weather. And if I do get caught, it'll be good for me to have a few needless murders under my belt. Makes me out to be a completely crazy fucker. That's the difference between hard time and a nice state hospital. Nurses, heavy barbiturates. That's how we save our asses up here. We just tell folks we're loco."

He waited for a moment. "Nothing to say, smart ass?" He waited again. "OK, then, say goodbye to Mommy."

On the deck of the cockpit she could see nothing, could only feel the heavy moist flakes landing on her face and the stabbing pain in her arm and back. And she could hear the metallic click of the firing mechanism over her head, followed by Kara's wailing: "No, no." Then the splash. His curse, and the slap of his hands on the wheel.

Suddenly, below the sound of the sailboat's engine, she detected something bigger and deeper—a powerful, throaty rumble. And then the snow-laden air was split by the majesty of an approaching foghorn.

Chuck clutched the metal edge of the control panel and tried to keep the dizziness from sending him sprawling across the blue metal deck. Tried to keep his trembling legs from buckling. Tried to keep from vomiting with each lurch of the boat through the violent gray swells. This is bad, he thought. I am worse than useless in this.

The snow would have been impenetrable for most men, but Gromek was used to picking his way through it and rain and worse. He steered with one hand and cupped the binoculars and the handset in the other.

"We have one overboard. The girl is overboard. I think

she jumped. Art is at the wheel. I think he was chasing her and now he's more worried about us. The woman is at his feet. She looks hurt. Over."

"I copy you, Captain." The voice belonged to a woman at the Coast Guard office, who had taken over the radio when Lyle and the others scrambled down to the boats. "Do not attempt to interfere with the sailboat," she said. "Help will be there shortly. Can you assist the girl? Over."

"We can try. Over."

"She's not such a great swimmer," Chuck said.

Gromek shook his head. "Doesn't much matter. When it's this cold, she's only got a few minutes until hypothermia sets in." He pulled back on the power and angled the ferry closer to shore. "She's too strong, damn it. She's going in too shallow." He grabbed another handset from overhead. "What's her name?"

"Kara."

"Kara!" Gromek's voice boomed over the snowy water from a huge bullhorn. "Kara, listen. Stay put. Tread water. I can't reach you if you get in any closer."

Art's first shot zinged off the metal below the windows of the pilothouse. "Jesus H. Christ." Gromek swore, then shook the pistol out of his jacket pocket. Another shot boomed in the snowy wind, and Gromek swore again. "He's firing on the girl now. Here." He handed the pistol to Chuck. "Keep him busy. I'll try to get the ship between him and her." As he handed the gun over, he looked at it, and into Chuck's eyes, but he didn't hesitate. "Get out there, damn it. Shoot him."

The snow whipped Chuck's face as he stepped into it. He crouched behind the metal railing, feeling the gun in his still-aching hands. Another shot cracked the air, ricocheted off the ferry hull. Chuck tried to aim the pistol down at Art, now thirty yards off to his left, now twenty-five as Gromek moved to shield Kara. The shot seemed impossible: the ferry rolled, the sailboat was bobbing wildly, and Gretchen still lay at Art's feet as Chuck looked down. The water heaved violently, and the fear rose up in him, paralyzed him. He closed his eyes and ducked behind the railing.

"Shoot him. Shoot the fucker." Gromek's voice boomed out of the bullhorn.

He pulled himself up. With his arm braced on the vibrating railing, he sighted on the cockpit, not fifteen yards away. He fought back the nausea and fired. Twice. Gromek pulled closer, now directly between Kara and the sailboat, and jammed the ferry into reverse. He was going back for her, and the sailboat would begin to pull away. Chuck aimed, fired, missed. Art fired again and the windowpane behind Chuck exploded.

He ducked, the glass dancing in the snowy air, and when it was gone he raised his head. The sailboat was moving away and then, abruptly, Gretchen was on one knee. One arm hung limply at her side but the other was flailing, now pulling at Art's arm as he tried to aim, now grappling at the wheel, now at his legs.

He turned and stomped on her.

For an instant his broad back was fully squared to Chuck and in that same instant the sailboat rode to the crest of a wave and balanced there. The vibration of the ferry faded to a low hum. A million feathery wisps of snow parted and he fired through them.

Art slammed forward, clutched at the wheel and then fell, one arm draped over a lifeline. As he let go of the wheel the boat lurched, then motored off on a new course.

Three hundred yards ahead of it lay a coven of black, wave-battered rocks. No one moved in the cockpit.

Gromek saw what had happened and now the ferry shook violently as he shoved it into forward again and throttled up. "Get ready to jump," he said over the bullhorn. "Steer it out into the channel."

"No." Chuck pleaded to him through the blasted window of the pilothouse. "No. I can't do that."

"You jump or you lose her. And don't screw around. That little girl's gonna freeze soon." Chuck shook his head. "Go, you fucking waterboy. Go now."

Chuck scrambled down the wet metal stairs, slipping, catching himself, slipping again. Halfway down, he reached the high wall around the ferry deck and leaned against it. He threw one leg over, straddling it, but could not look at the roiling water. He clenched his eyes against the spray, until he heard Gromek's voice above him. "Go now!" it thundered, and he raised his eyes.

The sailboat was three feet from him, then six feet as it slipped down a gully in the waves, then four feet. He grabbed the stair railing and pulled himself up, using his arms more than his trembling legs. He took two shaky breaths and timed the jump not to the roll of the sailboat but to the ebb and flow of his courage. He felt it rise in him and he leaped over the frigid lake water and crashed headlong against the hull—one arm catching on the rear stay, the other clawing the foamy air. One foot hit the slick hull; the other went underwater up to the thigh. He pulled on the stay and struggled for a foothold but slid off. The ferry was already reversing, away from the rocks, back toward Kara. He slipped again. Then he pulled fiercely on the stay and gave a heart-popping adrenaline kick against the hull and he was sprawling in the cockpit next to Gretchen.

He heard her groan and bent to her. He lifted her head off the slats and spoke to her. She said nothing. He spoke again, but in the next moment heard the grind of granite across fiberglass. He grabbed the wheel and twisted it toward the channel. The boat rose on a wave, came down with a sickening thunk and grind, and then fell off. The next wave raised them and pushed them back, away from the black pyramids. The boat leaned heavily for an instant and he thought that it was sinking. "Oh, my God," he cried. Then it righted itself and made headway under power.

Gretchen moaned and stirred again. "Don't move, honey," he said. He wanted to bend down to her but was afraid to release the wheel. So he talked. "Stay there. Don't move."

She opened her eyes. Her hand rose up to her face and wiped away the melted snow and through her sobs she cried out, "Kara. Kara."

He looked back over his shoulder, and at the top of the next wave saw that Gromek was now in the door of the pilothouse. Chuck followed the rope from the old man's hand to the water, to the red-orange life preserver, to Kara, who was now grabbing it. Gromek pulled her steadily toward the ferry, tied off the line, then leaped down the metal steps to her.

A huge wave crashed over the sailboat then, pushing it down. Water flowed into the cockpit and down into the cabin. Gretchen gagged and desperately jerked her head up. He twisted the chrome wheel into the waves now, but too late to avoid the next one. He held on tightly, dropped his eyes to Gretchen, then looked up to see Art's wounded body catch for an instant on the jib line, then wash over the side. Chuck screamed and stretched out for it, grabbing nothing. As the next wave crested he saw the body gently dancing in its peak. Then it disappeared.

Gretchen was sitting up now, coughing. Chuck looked back again and Gromek was not visible. Then he saw her, Kara, at the railing in Gromek's old plaid coat. A moment later he heard the foghorn, twice, its sound deep and ancient and cheering.

# Bartok

*I've been robbed.*

*Wilkerson says otherwise, and he can give me all the damn reasons in the world why the money should be gone. But confusing people is a lawyer's job. You never put stock in what they say. Especially when he was the bagman and he's worried that someone might suspect him of having the money. He wants everyone to think the money is gone. That way, no one's going to come knocking on his door.*

*I'm not confused about that. Wilkerson doesn't have the balls to steal from me. Cancel that. He doesn't have the balls to steal from me and hang around here. He knows he'd get tripped up eventually and I'd rip his fat friggin' arms out. But he is sticking around. So he didn't take the money.*

*But someone did.*

*Wilkerson and Lyle keep saying it's a haircut. Everyone got trimmed and what was there ain't there no more.*

"You've rejected the banking system," Wilkerson said, "but you still think you're entitled to insured investments."

For that, I should have popped the fat prick.

Haircut my ass. I know better. Even if I hadn't been listening to Leo at the end, when what came out of his mouth was about half words and half drool, I wouldn't be fooled by this. What he said only confirms it. Not that he said exactly that he took it. But if you listen closely, that was the meaning.

What he said was that a smart person would know that something stinks. So I asked him what, and he leaned over to me, so close that his damn skanky beard was lying on my neck. "What you smell," he whispered, "is the decomposing body of God." And then he laughed like a friggin' loon.

I think what he meant was that he had done something horrible, betrayed his own best side. By taking the money, he'd killed God. Right. Like a sorry old broken-down s.o.b. like Leo had the power to kill God.

I told him, "Leo, God ain't dead. Earth has been here a couple hundred million years, God's never even had a standing eight count." I said, "God don't stink. People do. God's going to be around for a long time, and so am I, and we both want to know where the money is."

He waved his arms around and said, "When I die, everything dies."

Some preacher.

Everyone else wants to put this behind them. They feel horrible about Art flipping out and killing Brian and Jeanine. And maybe Mrs. Ford. They feel terrible about Blaylock. They just feel all torn up inside.

Tough titties. I want my money.

# Twenty-three

He'd forgotten how much he knew about smuggling.

He'd never carried pot across an international border, but it had been a subject of some conversation over the years. From grass hovels on Koh Samui to vile hotels outside the old city in Fez to Cay Caulker in Belize, everyone had a story. Joints in shirt seams, hash balls in salt shakers, bales wrapped and weighted and dragged behind sailboats by a wire that could be cut at the first sign of a Coast Guard vessel. In a hostel in Accra, he'd met two Canadians who were collecting exotic snakes for a pet store in Toronto. They'd stuck a pound of local marijuana in a sack with a spitting cobra, confident that the smell of snake feces would put off even the most discerning canine. And even if the dog barked, it would take the most dedicated agent to open the sack.

He had smuggled money before, during his months in Ghana. All the travelers made regular trips to the black market money traders in Togo, to trade U.S. dollar traveler's checks for Ghanaian cedis at double the official rate. One night he'd slipped an inch-thick wad of cedis into his sock and walked across the border to find that the last truck-bus had departed. He'd hitched a ride with a family who—at the third army roadblock—admitted they were trafficking black market goods. That began a long night of interrogation by teenagers with automatic weapons, but he'd kept his cool and his money.

Next to that, it would be easy to get this $60,000 back home. He thought about stuffing it behind a door panel, but that seemed unnecessarily complicated. And he had visions of a fender bender that could unhinge the door and pop the panel, littering the countryside with the down payment on his house.

In the end, he did the simple thing. He opened the trunk that held his old inlaid boxes, unwrapped the biggest two, and filled them with hundred-dollar bills. He wrapped them back in tissue paper, put them at the bottom of the trunk, and hefted it into the back of the station wagon. He packed their clothes around the trunk, and a box of books that Gretchen had selected. The lion's-paw throne was lashed onto the roof.

The air felt clean and bracing. He felt strong and rested and ready for the ferry. Vengeance is the Lord's, he said. And I am but His humble servant.

The pain was not as bad as it had been, but Gretchen thought it was worse than it should be. She worried that she might have suffered internal injuries the Bayfield doctor had missed.

She worried that Chuck would not be able to drive onto the ferry or, once on, wouldn't be able to drive off.

She worried that Kara would dump the bike on the highway. They had argued about that, and Kara had revealed that she'd not only ridden on motorcycles but actually driven them. She was utterly confident of her skills, utterly contemptuous of Gretchen's refusal. This is a different girl, Gretchen thought. She's been changed by this, and you will never change her back. You are still her mother but you are also, now, her accomplice.

And what *does* Penelope Leach say about this? she asked herself.

They had talked frequently about the events of the previous week. Chuck said they should approach it like recovering alcoholics, a day at a time. He wanted them to talk about it every day for as long as it took. As soon as he said it, she knew it was an inspired strategy. They needed to work it over so often, in such detail, that it became mundane. Not a secret so much as tired family lore. It would make the story less glamorous. It would eliminate the urge to tell others.

Maybe. Sort of. Good luck.


With the helmet and the bomber jacket and the snowmobile mittens and a warm sun shining on the highway, she could sit back and enjoy the ride. She had learned about motorcycles on newer models, in the city. She had learned on the sly, from friends and boyfriends, without her mother's knowledge or approval; that this revelation could cause a minor blowout, only a week after they had been shot at and nearly drowned, struck Kara as a sign that they were both on the mend.

This was different. The bike's heavy solidity, the deep bass throbbing of the engine, the winding, pine-braced, empty highway—this was where the mystique had started. This, she thought, is why they wrote those road songs. She leaned gently into the curve behind the pine trees and twisted up the throttle. Just a hair. Nothing to alarm her mother and Chuck, who were trailing in the Subaru. The time to air it out would come later, when they got it home.

First to the ferry, treating the bike as though it could detonate at any minute. Then to the U-Haul in Bayfield. Then you give it up for the tow home. And you give it up for the winter. Then a few incidental trips to the mall. To the supermarket. Then . . . Wyoming.

She pulled over in front of the store and firmly planted her left foot before climbing off. This was critical. After driving well, she didn't want to lose points by dumping a stopped bike.

The Subaru pulled up behind her as she slid off the helmet. Chuck got out first. He lowered his sunglasses, winked at her, and said (loud enough for her mother to hear), "Good job. A little fast on the first curve. But not bad."

Gretchen got out slower, her face still badly bruised. Her muscles still ached and she was still not comfortable with the cast on her arm. "Just don't get too used to it," she said sternly. "That is not your bike. And never will be."

"Damn straight," Chuck said. He started for the store.

"I don't even like it," Kara protested. "It's old and clunky."

Both adults went into the store and she waited for them at the curb, taking what she hoped would be a last look around the village. A silver truck pulled up and parked on the other side of the street. Lyle Pointer got out, looked intently up and down the street even though nothing was moving for three hundred yards in any direction. He ran his thumbs along the top of his belt, as if to confirm that it was still there, then nodded to her. She nodded back. Then the door on the other side of the pickup opened and Bartok stepped out. He started walking around the truck bed but Lyle said something to him and he stopped.

Lyle shambled over. "Your folks inside?"

"Yeah."

"You're on your way now?"

"Yeah." She had no desire to sound like an irritable teenager, but she couldn't think of anything to say.

"I don't expect any of you will be rushing back here."

She shrugged. "I guess not." We may be moving far away, she thought. We may be buying freaking Versailles. She glanced across the street at Bartok, who was picking his teeth with a fingernail. He glared back at her, his eyes half lidded. You jerk, she thought, if you only knew.

She didn't want to take the money but went along for her parents' sake. She couldn't see how it would improve her life. It meant moving away from the few good friends she had, to a suburban school where she would be treated like the AFS student from Ghettoland. But her mother and especially Chuck wanted the money. And there was the justice issue. Like Chuck said: Would you give back lost gold to Pol Pot?

"But it's still stealing, isn't it?" she'd asked.

"No," he'd said. "It's the spoils of war. It isn't right or wrong. It's what you get when your side wins."

Pointer looked away now, then leveled his eyes at her.

"I want you to know two things. First, we're not as bad as all this must have appeared. The circumstances have been unlike anything that anyone has seen up here in a hundred years. This is the kind of thing that will be talked about for generations."

Right, she thought. This is a regular Mayberry.

"Second, I want you to know I think you're a tough little cookie. You impressed a lot of people around here."

"Thanks," she said, wincing.

"It's not part of my job, really, to say this. I'm just here to stop crimes, or solve them once they've happened. So don't think of me as a cop doing this. So, as a personal observation, I'm impressed. And, of course, I'm sorry for what you people have been through. Especially you."

She nodded and thought she should say something in response, but felt paralyzed. And patronized: Why me more than my mother, who nearly had her face split open? she wondered. Why me more than Chuck, or dead Jeanine, or Brian, or poor refried Blaylock? Then the door swung open behind her and she heard Chuck's voice. "Lyle."

Lyle's hands went back to his belt. "Hi, Chuck. So you're all packed up?"

"On the next ferry."

"Good." He nodded absently, then raised his eyebrows as Gretchen pushed through the glass door. "Hi."

"Hi." Her mother might have tried to smile or it might have been a snarl. With her face so wrecked every expression looked like a nasty twitch.

"Say," Lyle began. "I don't mean to trouble you now, but try to keep in touch. We'll need to know where you are for the next couple of months at least. And if we ever find what he did to Mrs. Ford, we might need you again."

Chuck nodded solemnly. "You're sure she's not just visiting someone off the island? A friend . . . ?"

Kara was astonished at his calm, and his faith that neither she nor her mother would falter. He could talk about the dead woman offhandedly, she thought, then switch to football, then back to Mrs. Ford—all without a stammer. She had known that ugly secrets were a commonplace. Now, she thought, I know how families keep them. You have trust that the guilt will keep you together. You have faith in the sin.

"Maybe," Lyle went on. "She's also got a sister in Washington we haven't been able to find yet. But under the circumstances, I'm not optimistic. Maybe she saw Art dragging Jeanine down the beach. Maybe he didn't like what she was wearing that day. We'll never know."

"As soon as you hear from her, or find out what happened, let me know," Chuck said. "If she shows up and wants to stay in the house, it's rightfully hers." Here, Chuck hesitated, looked away and then back at Lyle. "If she doesn't show up, I guess we'll get Wilkerson to put it up for sale. But there's no rush."

Behind them, Kara saw old Gromek step out of the restaurant toward them. He was wearing the same plaid wool coat he'd given her on the boat. She had kept it wrapped around her the rest of that morning, holding it like a talisman against the cold, insisting that the Coast Guard officers pile the blankets over it until she was inside. Later, a gaggle of old women from the village had taken over. She'd stripped off her wet clothes but insisted on putting the coat back on, the tattered silky lining against her bare skin. She thought she had slept in it at one point. She had no idea how Gromek had gotten it back.

"Morning," he said. Then he excused himself, trying to pass by without talking.

"Morning, Mr. Gromek," she said.

He nodded at her and kept moving between them.

"Excuse me." Chuck raised an open hand at him, and Gromek stopped. "We're going now and I was afraid I might not have a chance to talk on the ferry. I just wanted to thank you again."

He lowered his hand, and Gromek glared at it, horrified that Chuck might extend it to him to shake. When Chuck stuck his hand in his jacket pocket, the old man's face relaxed.

"I'm sorry all of you had to go through it," Gromek said. "I'm sorry for Jeanine and Mrs. Ford and everyone on the island. This is our home, you know." He clutched his arms over his chest. "But it only changes so much. I'm not a sentimental man. When all this dies down and the horror of what Art did goes away, I'll still think poorly of you. You betrayed us all. Because of cowards like you, some of our boys died. That's a kind of treason and if it were up to me you'd be punished for it. Even today."

He pushed through them then and walked down toward the pier. No one on the sidewalk spoke. The features on her mother's face moved. If her lips had been working properly, Kara thought, her mother would have spit.

Finally, Chuck said it was time to get the car on the ferry. Lyle nodded and backed away. Kara noticed—with relief—that they didn't shake hands either.

"Mom, can I borrow a few bucks? I need to put some gas in this old hog," Kara said.

"It's not a hog," Chuck said. "It's a Triumph."

Gretchen slipped her purse off her shoulder and handed it over. "There's some in the side pocket. Otherwise give them a credit card."

She threw the purse over her shoulder, kicked the bike into life, mounted, gave it a little taste of gas. Under her, she could hear the delicious rumble of power just barely under control. I could definitely learn to like this, she thought. She left her helmet off, throttled up. The bike carried her fifty yards down the street, then traced a broad arc into the Amoco pumps.

She gave the ribbed, chrome gas cap a good twist but nothing happened. Bending toward it, she noticed the keyhole for the first time. That can't be stock, she thought. She slipped the key ring out of the ignition, turned it over in her hand—only one key, obviously too big.

Befuddled, she stood for a moment, then looked up the street for Chuck. She would lose points asking for help if the solution was obvious, so she waited, considering how else the tank might be filled, where else the key might be kept.

The next instant she remembered the key her mother had found in Leo's office, the one that looked like it might belong to a safety-deposit box. Of course, she thought, and her assurance that it would work was absolute. She rummaged through the purse until she picked out the small manila envelope. She dropped the key into her hand, slipped it into the gas cap. It twisted with an oily click; she gave the gas cap a half turn and it came free.

She grabbed the dull steel nozzle from the pump and inserted it. The gas splashed noisily in the tank, then softer as it filled. She glanced down the street. Lyle had disappeared but Bartok still leaned against the side of the truck, shifting one way, then the other, like a bear scratching its back on a tree trunk. He eyed her as he moved.

Please don't let him come over here, she thought. She hung the gas nozzle back on the pump and then—as she started to rethread the gas cap—it caught her eye. At first she thought it was a strange reflection off the fuel, then maybe an oil slick. Then she saw the hard edges and knew that it was an object, or rather the corner of an object, a plastic bag in fact, floating on the gas. She dipped a finger deep into the tank, slipped it under the bag, lost it, and fished it up again, this time through the opening and onto the tank's blue metal.

A plastic bag, yes, taped round and round. And in it, a woman's watch on a narrow black band. She looked down the street and didn't see Bartok. She turned it over and over and thought then to look at the face. Under the smashed crystal, the hands said 8:35. A little window was set in where the 3 should have been and in it she read "31."

Eight-thirty on New Year's Eve, she thought. Like he'd said. He'd been straight about the lie.

She trembled once, then slipped the bag into the pocket of the old bomber jacket. She reset the gas cap, twisted it tight, walked inside, and set a five-dollar bill before the old attendant. He gave her back a quarter and two dimes and told her to wait a second. She looked out and saw Bartok, now just twenty feet from the pumps.

"That's OK," she said. She moved out the door as quickly as possible without running and jumped onto the motorcycle's worn leather seat.

"Hey, wait a minute," Bartok said.

She started the bike and rocked it off the kickstand. He said something else, but she gunned the engine and drowned out his words. She was about to pop it into gear but he stepped in front of the bike and grabbed the handlebars.

"Just a minute," he said. "I think you've got something of mine."

"I don't know what you're talking about."

"Never hose a hoser," he said. "Didn't your mama teach you that?"

"Let go of this bike or I'll run you down."

"Try it and I'll throw you and this bike on the pavement." He grinned broadly, showing matched rows of straight, tea-colored teeth. "Look. I just want to know where my money is." The grin relaxed into a smirk. "Is that so unfair?"

"There was no money."

"Yes there was," he growled. "Leo kept it. He pretty much said so at the end."

"Leo was nuts."

"Either you tell me where it is, or I'm going to have to conduct my own search. And I'm going to start by patting you down, cupcake. First time I saw you, I wondered what you were hiding under those big sweaters."

"The threat of physical contact doesn't intimidate me," she said sternly. Then she smiled at him—a wide devilish smile—and raised her arms straight above her head, bent at the wrist, palms up like a chickie-girl in a perfume ad. "I have been patted before."

He didn't take the bait, but she confused him enough so that he relaxed his grip on the handlebars, and in that instant she kicked the bike into gear. When it lurched, he stumbled back reflexively, and in that instant she throttled up and pulled away. He grabbed at the bike and almost dumped it—but didn't.

She sped down the street, worried that he'd follow her. Down the block she could see that Chuck had turned the car and was waiting for her before he got in the ferry line. Lyle stood by his truck. He was talking to Wilkerson, the lawyer, who froze in mid-sentence to stare at her. He was hatless, but his trim brown topcoat was buttoned up to the neck.

Kara slowed down now, sure that Bartok wouldn't run past Lyle to get her. She pulled up behind the Subaru, then followed as Chuck drove by the store and Laundromat, onto the cement pier. A double line of cars and trucks ran up to the ferry.

The gate was down but a young man was waving his arms in an X, telling the drivers not to drive on board. He walked off the ferry now, between the idling cars. He spoke to the drivers as he walked by. When he got to her, he said, "It'll be a few minutes. Gromek's disappeared."

"Sure." She glanced up the street, assured herself that Bartok was not coming, then walked up to the Subaru on Chuck's side. She leaned in the window. "Gromek went back for more doughnuts, I guess. Guy says it'll be a minute."

Chuck looked ahead, at the line of cars and trucks, and said nothing.

"How you doing?" she asked. "You gonna be able to get on and off?"

"I don't have much of a choice, do I?" He swallowed, then smiled weakly up at her.

She reached into the jacket, wrapping her hand around the plastic bag. She grinned at him, thinking of the power she held over him. He grinned back nervously and sighed. "When we get over to Bayfield, don't get too far ahead of me or anything," she said.

"You afraid I'm going to run off?"

"This would be the time to do it, wouldn't it?" she teased him. "You got the money. You leave the kid in your dust. Forget your wife at the next gas station. After all, she has grown suddenly less attractive, don't you think?"

"Oh, that's nice," her mother snapped. "I get my head crushed and that's the sympathy I get."

"Sorry," Kara said. "You're always pretty to me, Mom." She hesitated. "You know you can't run off. We know too much."

"It would only mean I'd have to run far, far away," he said. "But I already went there." He lowered his voice. "Nothing you know could make me stay, but you don't have to make me." He patted her hand and Gretchen's. Gretchen flinched and groaned.

"How long till we get going?" she asked.

"You got the time, Kara?" he asked.

"No," she said.

Her mother wiggled her wrist out of her sleeve, and moaned, "Nine-fifteen."

Kara stood, her hand still in the jacket. "I'll be back in a minute," she said.

She walked to the edge of the pier and watched the gulls cut and swoop above the boats. She would tell him, but later. Now she wanted to take care of this, immediately, on her own. She had the power to keep this bad thing away from her family, and she intended to exercise it.

She put her left foot forward, pulled the watch out of

the plastic bag. She held it a second, then cocked her arm, then lofted the tiny piece of metal on the frayed strap. She followed it with her eyes, but saw no splash as it slid beneath the rough cold water.